Heartland

❧

Come What May

by Lauren Brooke

SCHOLASTIC INC.

New York Toronto London Auckland Sydney
Mexico City New Delhi Hong Kong

With special thanks to Linda Chapman

*To the five gray horses that have touched my life —
enriching it beyond measure*

No part of this publication may be reproduced in whole or in part, or stored in a retrieval system, or transmitted in any form or by any means, electronic, mechanical, photocopying, recording, or otherwise, without written permission of the publisher. For information regarding permission, write to Scholastic Inc., Attention: Permissions Department, 555 Broadway, New York, NY 10012.

Library of Congress Cataloging-in-Publication data available.

ISBN 0-439-13026-3

Heartland series created by Working Partners Ltd, London.

Copyright © 2001 by Working Partners Ltd.
Published by Scholastic Inc. All rights reserved.

SCHOLASTIC and associated logos are trademarks and/or registered trademarks of Scholastic Inc. HEARTLAND is a trademark and/or registered trademark of Working Partners Ltd.

12 11 10 9 8 7 6 5 4 3   1 2 3 4 5 6/0
Printed in the U.S.A.   40
First Scholastic printing, March 2001

Chapter One

❧

A cold November wind blew across the training ring, tossing Amy Fleming's light-brown hair in all directions. She hardly noticed. All her attention was focused on the black mare cantering around her. Seeing Gypsy begin to slow, Amy pitched the coiled line in the direction of the mare's hindquarters.

"Go on!" she urged.

Gypsy snorted and plunged forward again, her hooves thudding into the damp sand, the muscles rippling under her shining coat. Amy watched intently, moving in the center, so that her shoulders stayed square to the horse's.

After two more circles around the ring, Gypsy's inside ear flopped slightly, the point of it seeming to fix on Amy, and then her head and neck came down toward the ground, her mouth opening and closing.

Amy recognized the signal. In her own language — the language of gesture and body positioning — the mare was saying that she wanted to cooperate. Dropping the rope to her side, Amy broke eye contact and turned her shoulders sideways to the horse. It was time to show that she was no threat — to invite the mare to be a team with her.

Gypsy's hooves slowed down and stopped. Amy waited. There was a long pause, and then she heard the plod of the mare's hooves as she began to move toward her. Amy held her breath. Suddenly the mare appeared at her side. Her soft muzzle reached out and touched Amy's shoulder.

It was join-up! Delight surged through Amy as she slowly turned and rubbed Gypsy's lowered forehead.

Join-up was a technique that Amy had learned from her mom, Marion. By communicating with horses in their own language, a bond based on trust and understanding could be developed between horse and human. At Heartland, the equine sanctuary that Marion had set up to cure physically and emotionally damaged horses, join-up was the first stage of treatment. Before her death five months ago, Amy's mom had used join-up on all the horses that came to Heartland.

Amy turned away from Gypsy and walked across the ring. The mare followed. Wherever Amy went, so did the horse. Stopping at last, Amy turned toward the gate where Ty, Heartland's seventeen-year-old stable hand, was watching.

"Well, what do you think?" she called to him, clipping the longline onto Gypsy's halter.

"She's doing really well," Ty replied. He swung himself over the gate and came across the ring to meet her, the wind ruffling his dark hair. "She's a different horse from when she arrived," he said, patting the black mare.

Amy nodded. Five-year-old Gypsy belonged to a dressage rider named Pamela Murray. The horse had arrived at Heartland two months ago, nervous and uncooperative and with a bad habit of launching into a series of corkscrew bucks when she got excited. Working together, Amy and Ty had treated her nervousness by using aromatherapy oils and Bach Flower Remedies and had then encouraged her to cooperate through join-up. Gradually Gypsy had relaxed and become less stubborn. She hadn't bucked now for more than three weeks, and each time Amy joined-up with her, the process seemed to occur more quickly and smoothly.

Amy looked at Gypsy nuzzling the collar of Ty's coat. "Do you think she's ready to go back to Pamela's yet?"

A frown crossed Ty's deep green eyes. "I'm not sure. I know she's been behaving, but I'm still not convinced that she won't try bucking again. And if she does and manages to throw her rider, then we'll be back to square one, because she'll have learned that bucking works."

"You're right," Amy agreed, "I feel that way, too." She smiled at him, glad that their instincts were the same. Since the road accident that had killed her mom, Amy had shared all the decisions about the horses with Ty. Apart from one awful moment when she had thought he was going to leave Heartland, they had always gotten along well together, and Amy knew that she owed him a lot. Without Ty, she doubted whether Heartland could have kept going. While he helped her treat the horses, Amy's grandpa, who owned Heartland farm, looked after the house and the land, and Lou, Amy's older sister, took care of the business side of things.

"I'll call Pamela today," Ty said, "and explain that we need to keep Gypsy a while longer." He opened the gate and they led the mare down to her stall.

As they passed the back barn, tall, blond Ben Stillman, Heartland's new stable hand, appeared, pushing a laden wheelbarrow. Seeing them, he stopped. "How did Gypsy do today?"

"Good, thanks," Amy replied.

"All six stalls in the stable block have been mucked out," Ben said efficiently. "And I've done four of the ones up here," he said, nodding toward the twelve-stall barn.

"I'll come and give you a hand with the rest," Ty said.

"Me, too," Amy said, feeling slightly guilty that Ben had been working. "I'll just sort Gypsy out."

Just then, the back door of the farmhouse opened, and Lou came out. "Breakfast's ready!" she shouted.

Amy thought about the muffins, eggs, and ham that would be waiting inside the house for them. "We can finish the stalls after breakfast," she said quickly to Ty and Ben, her stomach starting to rumble. Her grandpa always cooked a big breakfast for everyone at Heartland on Saturday mornings in the winter. "Come on," she said, leading Gypsy forward. "Let's go in."

Ty fell into step beside her, but Ben stayed by the wheelbarrow. Amy glanced over her shoulder. "Aren't you coming, Ben?"

"I think I'll pass," Ben said.

Amy stopped in surprise. "What? You're going to skip one of Grandpa's famous breakfasts?"

Ben shrugged. "There's too much to do. I'll finish up the stalls." He must have seen Amy's astonished expression. "It's no big deal. I'm really not hungry." Taking hold of the handles of the wheelbarrow, he headed up the yard toward the muck heap. "See you later," he called.

Amy looked at Ty. It wasn't the first time that week that Ben had refused to take a break.

Ty raised his eyebrows. "You heard him," he said. "We can't make him eat breakfast if he doesn't want to."

"But he's working so hard," Amy said as they walked Gypsy back to her stall.

"We can't really complain," Ty replied dryly. "Just think how he used to be."

Amy thought back to when Ben had first arrived at Heartland a month ago. He had been sent to work at the horse sanctuary by his aunt, Lisa Stillman, who owned a large Arabian stable. She had thought training at Heartland would be a great opportunity for Ben. At first, Ben had been skeptical of the alternative therapies and training methods used at Heartland. He didn't offer to help at all. However, since Ty and Amy had saved Red, Ben's beloved showjumper, from poisoning, he had started to make much more of an effort.

But he's doing almost too much, Amy thought. "It's like he's working so hard to make up for the way he was at first," she said out loud, opening Gypsy's door.

"At least it gets the work done," Ty said.

"Ty!" Amy exclaimed, but she wasn't totally surprised by his comment. When Ben hadn't been pulling his weight, Ty was the one who had to do the extra work. And even though things had improved a little since Ben had lost his attitude, Amy had a feeling it was going to be some time before Ty and Ben considered each other friends.

As Amy came out of the stall, Ty bolted the door, and the two of them headed down to the old clapboard farmhouse. They kicked off their boots and went into the warm kitchen. The smell of freshly brewed coffee and homemade muffins hung in the air.

Jack Bartlett, Amy and Lou's grandpa, was standing by the stove, stirring a pan of fluffy scrambled eggs. He looked up as they entered, his strong, weather-beaten face creasing into a smile. "Hungry?" he said.

"You bet!" Ty grinned.

"Can I do anything, Grandpa?" Amy offered.

"No, just sit down," Grandpa replied.

Lou was pouring out glasses of orange juice, her short golden-blond hair still mussed from sleep, her pale skin flushed pink from the heat of the kitchen. "Where's Ben?" she asked.

"Still out in the barn," Amy replied. "He wanted to keep working."

"We can't let him do that," Jack Bartlett said, a look of concern showing in his pale blue eyes. He took the pan off the heat. "Lou, go and call him."

"No, don't," Amy said hastily to her sister. "Besides, he said he wasn't hungry." She knew how stubborn Ben could be. Having made up his mind, nothing would change it. She had a feeling that if Lou tried to persuade him it would only cause a scene.

Lou looked at Grandpa uncertainly.

He ran a hand through his thinning gray hair. "OK," he said. "But next weekend, no excuses."

Amy picked up a plate of ham. "Is this ready to be put on the table?" she asked, changing the subject.

Grandpa nodded, spooning the pile of eggs into a

serving dish. "All right," he said. "Sit down, everyone. We're just about ready to eat."

Half an hour later, the dishes in the center of the table had been emptied and everyone's plates scraped clean. Amy put down her coffee mug and sighed contentedly. "That was great, Grandpa," she said.

"Yeah, Jack — one of the best," Ty agreed.

Grandpa smiled. "Glad you enjoyed it."

Just then, the phone rang. "I'll get it," Lou said, jumping to her feet and reaching for the handset. "Hello, Heartland, how may I help you?" Her voice suddenly became brisk and efficient.

There was a pause. Then Amy saw a look of concern cross her sister's face.

"I see," Lou said, her voice sounding serious. "Well, you are pretty far away. You don't know anyone else who could help, Mr. Phillips?"

Amy glanced at Ty. He raised his eyebrows. It sounded like whoever it was on the phone needed help with a horse.

"OK," Lou went on. "If you give me your number, I'll find out if we have room and get back to you as soon as possible."

"Who was that?" Amy asked as soon as Lou had replaced the phone.

"A guy named Ray Phillips," Lou said. "His wife died

recently, and he wants us to take on a mare that she kept at their farm over on Wilson's Peak. The mare's in foal, and he doesn't know much about horses."

"Wilson's Peak? It's fairly isolated over there," Jack commented.

Lou nodded. "That's why he wants to bring the mare over here. He doesn't think he can get her through the labor by himself."

"Of course, we'll take her," Amy said immediately. "Won't we, Ty?"

Ty nodded.

Grandpa frowned. "I thought all our stalls were full."

"Uh-uh. Charlie's being picked up by his owner this morning," Ty explained. "We were going to call the next name on the waiting list, but this mare sounds like she needs the stall more."

Amy turned to her sister again. "How pregnant is she?"

"Ten months," Lou replied.

"That means her foal is due in about four weeks," Ty calculated, looking concerned. "It's not a good idea for her to travel so late in her pregnancy."

"I guess Mr. Phillips doesn't have much choice," Lou said.

"Will you call him back, Lou?" Amy urged. "Tell him we'll take her right away."

"Sure," Lou said, picking up the phone.

"And ask him how tall she is and about her breeding. And find out her name," Amy added quickly as her sister punched in the number.

She waited impatiently while Lou spoke to Ray Phillips again.

"Well?" Amy demanded as soon as Lou hung up.

"Her name is Melody," Lou said, looking at the notes she had scribbled down. "She's seven years old, a fifteen-two liver-chestnut quarter horse. Mr. Phillips is going to bring her over this afternoon. He said he'll pay any veterinary fees and her feeding costs until we rehome her and the foal."

"I'm going to let Ben know," Amy said to Ty. She jumped to her feet, grabbed the two remaining muffins, and folded them into a napkin. "I'll take him these."

"Do you need a hand clearing the table, Jack?" Ty asked, looking around at the dirty plates.

Grandpa shook his head. "Thanks, but it's OK. You two can get back to the yard work."

"I can't wait for Melody to get here," Amy said as she and Ty pulled on their jackets and boots and hurried outside into the cold. "And for the foal to be born." Her mom had rescued several mares with young foals, but a foal had never actually been born at Heartland. "It's going to be so cool," she said. "Can you imagine how cute it will be?"

Ty glanced at her. "Just remember that it has to be re-homed as soon as it's old enough," he warned.

"I know," Amy said impatiently. It was one of the rules at Heartland — all horses were rehomed if they could be. It was only by sticking to this rule that new horses could be rescued or cured. But for now, she didn't want to think about that — she wanted to enjoy the thought of a foal cantering around the paddocks in the spring sunshine.

Ty saw her expression. "Oh, no, you're going to fall in love with it, aren't you?" he groaned.

Amy raised her eyebrows. "And you're not?"

"Me? Never!" Ty said.

Amy grinned. She knew Ty too well to believe him. He would adore a newborn foal as much as she would — if not more!

Just then, one of the stall doors opened in the front stable block and Ben came out. "I'm going to tell him the news," Amy told Ty.

She hurried over. "Hi!" she called, holding out the muffins. "I brought you these."

Ben unfolded the napkin. "Thanks," he said gratefully.

"We have some news." Amy eagerly told him about Melody. "She's coming after lunch. We can put her in Charlie's stall."

"Sure," Ben said, nodding. "It'll need to be cleaned and disinfected before Melody goes into it. We'll have to attach the water bucket to the wall so that she doesn't knock it over when she goes into labor. And after the foal comes we should remove the haynet — just to make sure the foal doesn't get caught in it." He stuffed the muffins in his pocket and set off up the yard.

"How do you know all this stuff?" Amy asked in surprise as she walked alongside him.

Ben shrugged his broad shoulders. "There were always foals being born at my aunt's place."

Amy thought about Lisa Stillman's stable with its modern barns and army of stable hands. Ben's mom had sent him to live there when he was twelve after she had gone through a difficult divorce with his father.

They reached the back barn. "I'll muck out the stall," Ben said.

Amy took Charlie's halter off the hook on his wall. "OK, I'll brush him so he's ready for his owner," she said, patting the palomino, who was looking out over the door. She knew she'd miss him when he returned home. He had been sent to Heartland to have his fear of trailers cured. Horses like Charlie and Gypsy, whose owners paid good money for them to be cured, made it possible for Heartland to rescue horses that needed help and had nowhere else to go.

Tying Charlie up in the aisle, Amy began to groom him.

"Are you still planning to take Red to that show at the fairgrounds in two weeks?" Amy asked Ben as he began to fork the straw from Charlie's bed into the wheelbarrow.

"I'm hoping to," Ben replied.

He had been practicing hard for the show, as it would be Red's first attempt at the High Prelim class. Red was only six years old, but he was very talented, and Amy knew that Ben dreamed of him one day becoming a Grand Prix showjumper.

"Are you going to be able to come and watch?" Ben asked her. "The class is in the afternoon. You can come in the trailer with me if you want."

"I'd love to," Amy said eagerly. Then she thought about her best friend, Soraya Martin. "I bet Soraya would like to tag along, too, if there's room."

"Sure, that would be great." Ben nodded.

Amy smiled to herself. Soraya thought that Ben was totally cute, and she'd definitely welcome the invitation. "How about your mom?" Amy asked, knowing that Ben's mom had originally planned to attend the show but had then called to say she couldn't make it. "She's still not coming?"

Glancing into the stall, she saw Ben's face tighten. "We haven't spoken since she canceled," he said.

Amy frowned. "How come?"

"Why should I call her?" Ben replied, scowling. "It's just a waste of time. She doesn't care what's going on with me."

"Ben!" Amy exclaimed. "She's your mom. Of course she does."

"You're wrong. All my mom's concerned about is winning her next case," Ben said, his voice suddenly bitter. "She's always been the same. When I was living at Fairfield, she was always too busy working to visit me. She's a lawyer first, a mom second."

"What? She never went to see you?" Amy said, shocked.

"Oh, at first she did," Ben said. "But then she came less and less." He shook his head. "I told you — she's too busy to care."

Amy frowned. She couldn't believe it. Nothing Ben's aunt had told them about his past had ever suggested that his mom was more interested in her career than she was in him. "It can't be that bad," she protested.

Ben stared at her for a long time. "How would you know what it's like, Amy? You couldn't possibly understand." Swinging around, he began forking through the straw with short, sharp movements.

Amy stared at his tense back for a moment. Then she turned away and began to brush out Charlie's tail. *How dare he say I don't understand,* she thought angrily. *At least his mom's still around. And she hasn't abandoned him — not entirely. Not like Daddy did.* Just thinking about her father made Amy upset. An international showjumper, he had been in a terrible accident on his horse twelve years ago that had ended his competitive career. Unable to cope, he had left Amy's mom, who brought up Amy and Lou on her own. They hadn't seen or heard from him since. Amy had been just three years old when he had left.

But that was forgetting the letter from England that she and Lou had found after their mom had died. It had been from their father. He had sent it five years ago, begging for a reconciliation. Amy didn't know if her mom had replied, but nothing had ever come of the correspondence.

Just then, Ben came out of the stall. "Look," he said, awkwardly shifting from foot to foot. "I'm sorry. I had no right to go off on you like that. I wasn't thinking about what I was saying."

Amy felt her frustration subside as she saw the genuine apology in his eyes. "Don't worry about it," she said. "Hey, listen — do you want to go for a ride at lunch?" she asked, suddenly eager to make up. "Sundance could use the exercise. We can make sure we're back by two o'clock, when Melody's due to arrive."

"OK," Ben said gratefully. "Sounds good to me."

It was windy out on the trails, but neither Sundance nor Red seemed to mind. They cantered along the tracks that led across Teak's Hill, the wooded slope that rose steeply behind Heartland. Amy was relieved that Ben seemed to have forgotten about the heated exchange they'd had that morning. He talked easily about the show and about his plans for Red. When he was in a mood like this, he was a lot of fun to be around, Amy thought. She just wished she could get him to lighten up more often.

They got back to Heartland just before two o'clock. "Hey, Scott's here," Amy said, seeing the local equine vet's battered Jeep parked in the driveway.

There was no sign of Scott around the barns, so Amy put Sundance away and went down to the house. She found Scott in the kitchen, talking to Lou.

"Hey, Amy," he said. "Lou called me and told me about the mare that's coming. I thought it might be a good idea to check her over when she arrives." He grinned at Lou. "Anyway, it was a great excuse to stop by."

Lou blushed and moved quickly to the sink.

Seeing her practical sister become flustered by Scott's comment, Amy smiled to herself. Lou and Scott had recently started dating.

"I think Melody's here," Lou announced, looking out the kitchen window. "I'll go get Grandpa. He's upstairs."

Amy glanced out the window to see an old wooden trailer pulling up beside Scott's Jeep. She hurried outside.

A tall man in his sixties, almost bald with stooped shoulders, was getting out of the pickup.

Amy went over. "Hi," she said. "I'm Amy Fleming."

"Ray Phillips," the man said slowly. "I've brought the mare — Melody."

He looked around in a vague manner, his eyes showing an absent look as if part of him were elsewhere.

Just then Grandpa came out of the house with Lou and Scott.

"This is Mr. Phillips," Amy said to Grandpa.

Grandpa shook hands and quickly introduced the other two.

"Thank you for agreeing to take Melody," Ray Phillips said. "I don't know what I'd have done if you'd said no. Things have been a bit of a strain." He looked almost helplessly at Jack. "Are you married, Mr. Bartlett?"

Amy saw a muscle leap in Grandpa's jaw in response to the abrupt question. "My wife died of cancer more than twenty years ago," he replied.

Ray Phillips shook his head. "I'm sorry."

"It was a long time ago," Grandpa said quietly, "and it gets easier."

Ray Phillips looked at the ground, seemingly in thought.

After a moment, Lou cleared her throat. "I guess we should get Melody out," she said, breaking the silence.

"Sandy — my wife — loved her so much," Mr. Phillips said. He sighed and glanced up. "Somehow I feel I'm betraying her by bringing Melody here."

"You're doing the right thing and what your wife would have wanted," Lou said gently. "We'll take good care of her, Mr. Phillips."

They were interrupted by the sound of restless hooves against the side of the trailer.

Scott went toward the ramp. "Did she travel OK?" he asked.

"She kicked around a bit," Ray Phillips replied. "She's always been nervous, but more so since she's been in foal. Sandy and I lived on our own, and Melody's only ever been used to being at our farm."

"Sure," Scott said reassuringly. He started to undo the bolts on the ramp. "OK, let's get her out."

Ty and Ben headed over from the barn. "Here, I'll give you a hand," Ty offered, hurrying to help Scott.

"Do you want me to lead her out for you?" Amy asked Mr. Phillips.

He hesitated before replying. "I don't know. It might be best if I do. I'm not sure how she'll react to a stranger going in there with her." He stepped into the box through the side door. There was a startled snort and the sound of hooves shying to one side. "Steady now," Amy heard Mr. Phillips say in a nervous voice.

Amy went to the door and glanced in cautiously. She

could just make out a high chestnut head with wide, startled eyes and pricked ears.

"It's OK," she murmured instinctively, stepping closer.

The frightened horse didn't seem to hear her. She was trembling.

"OK, we're bringing the ramp down," Scott called. "Just bring her out nice and steady, Mr. Phillips."

Suddenly Melody plunged backward. Ray Phillips gave a startled cry, and the rope slipped out of his hands.

"Watch out!" Amy cried in alarm. "She's loose!"

Dropping the ramp, Scott and Ty leaped out of the way just in time to avoid being trampled as the horse came shooting backward out of the trailer. The surface of the ramp was old and worn, and suddenly one of Melody's hind hooves slipped. With a startled whinny, she swung around. Catching sight of the whites of her frightened eyes, Amy lunged at the dangling lead rope, but she wasn't quick enough. The mare swerved and cantered straight toward Ben, her pregnant stomach swinging.

"Grab her, Ben!" Scott shouted.

Ben made a dive for the rope, but the mare shied out of his reach and he fell to the ground, his fingers grasping thin air.

With a terrified snort, Melody spun away from him. Already Ty was running to block off the driveway, but the mare wasn't heading for the drive. She was cantering in a blind panic straight toward the nearby paddock fence.

Amy saw her stride lengthen and suddenly realized that Melody was going to try to jump the fence. "No!" she gasped in horror. The mare was too heavily pregnant — she wouldn't make it!

Amy tried to run to cut her off but was already too late. At that moment, Melody gathered herself and took off.

For a fleeting second, Amy thought Melody was going to clear the fence, but the weight of her pregnant body dragged her down. Failing to make the height, she slammed into the top bar. It broke with a loud crack.

With a horrifying thud, Melody crashed awkwardly to the ground.

Amy ran harder, and as she closed in on the mare, her fears were confirmed. All she could see was the jagged end of the broken fence rail piercing deep into the horse's side.

Chapter Two

Flinging herself down on the grass, Amy frantically checked the mare for signs of life. Relief washed over her as she realized Melody was breathing hoarsely. Her eyes were open.

"Quick!" Amy cried out, seeing the others approaching. She stroked Melody's warm, damp neck. "It's OK, girl," she murmured, her heart hammering at the sight of the broken piece of wood sticking out of her side. "You're going to be just fine." She wished with all her heart that she could believe her own words.

Melody lifted her head and began to move her legs. "Stay still, girl," Amy said, desperately worried that if the mare tried to get up she might do herself more damage. But Melody had been disturbed by the sound of running footsteps, and she struggled unsteadily to her feet, her ears flicking nervously. Amy quickly took hold of the lead rope just as the others reached them.

"Oh, my God!" Ray Phillips exclaimed. "What happened? Look at her side!" He moved toward Melody, but Ty grabbed his arm.

"Please, it's best if you stay back, sir," he said quickly.

"She might panic if there are too many people around her," Scott explained as he opened his veterinary bag and knelt down by the mare. "Hold her still, Amy," he said quietly. "I'm going to sedate her so we can see exactly what the damage is."

Amy nodded as Scott filled a syringe from a bottle and glanced over his shoulder. "I'll need some hot water."

"I'll get it," Ben offered immediately.

"How bad is it?" Lou asked, sounding close to tears.

"I don't know yet," Scott replied, beginning to administer the injection. He looked around. "Ty, can you give Amy a hand holding Melody? I'm sedating her, but she's still shaky and she might well go down again."

Ty quickly joined Amy at Melody's head. Their gazes met for a moment. "It'll be all right," he said to her in a quiet voice.

Amy bit her lower lip, trying to hold back her tears. She couldn't cry now. She had to be strong for Melody's sake. She stroked the mare's trembling neck and swallowed hard.

As the drug started to take effect, Melody's head hung down and her eyes began to look glazed, the lids drooping. Her legs trembled, and suddenly she sank to her knees and her hindquarters thudded onto the grass. Scott pushed her over onto her good side and then crouched to examine the wound. Rivulets of blood were running over the taut skin of her belly from where the wood had pierced her side.

Amy felt sick as she thought about the foal. Was it hurt? But she knew she couldn't ask. Right now, the foal would be the last thing on Scott's mind; he would be concentrating on saving Melody. Without her, the foal stood no chance at this premature stage.

As Scott's experienced hands explored the gash, Amy glanced around at the others. The anxiety she felt was reflected in their faces. Grandpa had his arm tightly around Lou's shoulder, and Ray Phillip's face was ashen with shock.

Scott continued to examine the wound, gently feeling around the sharp splintered wood before running his hand quickly over her legs. "She's been lucky," he said, looking up at last, relief in his eyes. "She doesn't seem to have broken any bones, and the rail just missed her abdominal cavity. If that had been pierced it's unlikely we could have saved her. But I think I'll be able to patch this up. As long as her blood loss is minimal, her chances are good."

"So, she'll be OK?" Amy said, her hopes suddenly leaping.

Scott shook his head. "I can't say at this point. It's too early to tell. There's a possibility she'll pull through, but then she may still go into shock or into labor, and if the foal's born now it would have only the slimmest chance of survival." Before Amy could ask anything else, he opened his bag again and began to fire out rapid instructions. "Ty, I want you to monitor her pulse. Amy, stay by her head. Let me know if she shows signs of getting up, and keep checking her gums. If they get pale, let me know immediately — it could mean that she's going into shock." He looked around and saw that Ben had come back with the hot water. "Ben, can you watch her hindquarters, please? I need to know immediately if she goes into labor."

There was no time for questions. Everyone did as Scott had instructed. Amy crouched by Melody's head, her trembling hands gently smoothing and stroking the mare's face and cheeks. "Good girl," she murmured. "You're going to be just fine."

"OK," Scott said. "If everyone's ready, I'm going to start."

❧

It was a nerve-racking time, sitting by Melody's head while Scott used a local anesthetic in the mare's side. He gently eased the splintered wood out and then started cleaning the wound and removing the damaged tissue. Amy alternated between checking Melody's gums and massaging her ears. Her fingers worked in small circles as she concentrated on soothing the mare and keeping her still so that Scott could get on with his work unhindered. She tried not to look at the blood-soaked timber lying to one side. She tried not to think about Scott's earlier warning regarding blood loss. As Scott began to stitch up the injury, Amy glanced at Ty and Ben, dreading that at any moment one of them would say that something was wrong. Their faces were tense, but neither of them spoke.

At long last, Scott clipped the final suture and put down his scissors. "We're done," he announced. "I'll just give her a shot of antibiotics and a tetanus injection and then that's it. She can get back on her feet when she's ready. But it could take a while for the sedative to wear off."

Seeing him start to clear his things away, Lou, Grandpa, and Ray Phillips came over from the fence. Their faces were full of concern.

"Is Melody going to pull through?" Ray Phillips asked immediately.

Scott straightened up. "I hope so," he replied, wiping a hand across his forehead. "The wound's deep but shouldn't be life-threatening. She'll need very careful monitoring for the next week — antibiotic injections for at least two days and then powders in her food for another few days. Providing she doesn't go into shock, I think we can say she's had a lucky escape."

Amy asked the question that she couldn't hold back any longer. "What about the foal?"

"There's still a very real danger that Melody might go into labor at any time," Scott replied. "And like I said, if it does happen this early, the foal doesn't have a good chance of pulling through."

"But what about the fall? What if the foal was hurt?" Amy said anxiously.

Scott frowned. "It's impossible to know if the foal is OK, but it should have been well cushioned by the amniotic fluid and the walls of the uterus. We could scan Melody's belly to investigate, but I don't want to risk upsetting her. The calmer we can keep her, the better for both of them. Just keep a very careful eye on her. If she seems in discomfort or starts sweating or pacing around her stall, that might indicate the first stages of labor." Scott looked at the mare and shook his head. "The longer she can hang on to her foal, the better its chances of survival."

Just then, Melody lifted her head and neck. "OK, stand back, everyone," Scott said. "It looks like she's ready to get up."

"Should I unclip her lead rope?" Amy asked as Melody rolled shakily onto her stomach.

"No, you should stay with her," Scott replied as he and the others moved back. "Someone has to hold on to her in case she tries to get away. You've been talking to her for the last half hour — she's probably most comfortable with you."

Melody stretched out her front legs and, with a grunt of effort, struggled to her feet. She looked dazed and shaken. Seeing Amy, she snorted warily. Amy held out her hand. "Hey there, girl," she said.

Melody drew back, her ears flattening.

Remembering what her mom had taught her, Amy turned her shoulders sideways to the mare and made no attempt to approach her. Digging in her pocket she found a couple of mints. Careful not to alarm Melody by making direct eye contact, Amy offered one on the palm of her hand.

She waited. No one else made a sound.

With a cautious snort, Melody took a step toward Amy.

There was a pause, and then Amy felt the long whiskers on Melody's muzzle tickle her hand for an instant as the mare snatched the mint and backed off again. Amy still didn't move. Listening to the mare crunching the mint, Amy took the remaining one out of her pocket. She knew it was vitally important that Melody make the choice to approach her. If she walked up to the horse she would be seen as a predator, and the mare might try to escape.

Amy took a step away and held out the last mint. Holding her breath, she listened and waited and then heard the faint swish of Melody's hooves as she walked toward Amy and took it from her hand. This time she did not move away. In two crunches the mint was gone and Melody stepped closer to Amy, her soft muzzle exploring the pockets of Amy's jacket.

Slowly Amy turned and gently stroked the mare's forehead. Melody looked at her with wary dark eyes, but she accepted the caress and didn't move away. Amy heaved a sigh of relief. The first battle in gaining the mare's trust had been won.

❧

Melody was soon settled in Charlie's old stall. Although she seemed to be just about prepared to accept Amy, she was still nervous of everyone else.

"I'm sure she'll come around in time," Scott said as he and the others looked over the stall door. "I have to go now — but make sure you call me if you have any concerns. I'll drop by tomorrow morning to check her over and give her some more antibiotics. Make sure her bed is well cushioned. And bank up the straw around the edges — it'll protect her from rolling into the walls."

"We will," Amy promised.

"I can't believe all this is happening," Mr. Phillips said suddenly. Amy turned to look at him and could see that he was overcome with guilt. "I should never have tried to bring her over here in her condition," he continued. "It's all my fault. I should have just kept her at home and managed as best I could."

"You can't blame yourself," Scott said. "You did the right thing. In another month there could be snow, and you might have found yourself with a foaling emergency and no way for a vet to get out to you. She'll have the very best care here."

"But what if the foal's injured — dead even?" Ray Phillips said, shaking his head. "Sandy would be so upset, seeing Melody like this. I've let her down."

"No, you haven't," Lou said quickly. "Scott's right, Mr. Phillips, you did what you thought was best for Melody. I'm sure your wife would understand. You couldn't have known that this would happen."

"We'll look after her really well," Amy said to him.

Ray Phillips looked at them. "You've all been very kind. Thank you." He glanced into the stall. "You will let me know how's she's doing, won't you?"

"Of course," Lou said. "We'll call you regularly with news of her progress."

"And maybe when the foal's born you could come and visit," Grandpa suggested, stepping forward.

Ray Phillips nodded and then swallowed. "If everything's OK, of course," he said in a low voice.

"It will be," Amy said, wanting desperately to believe it.

He took one last look at Melody. " 'Bye, girl," he said, and then with the weight of guilt still etched into the lines of his face, he turned and walked slowly away. Grandpa and Lou followed.

"Poor guy," Scott said quietly.

Looking at the old man's bowed shoulders as he trudged toward his pickup, Amy nodded. What a horrible thing to have happened.

"I'll call tonight to see how she's doing," Scott said, glancing in at the mare. "But if you have any questions, call me right away."

"We will," Ty said. He walked down the yard with Scott, leaving Amy alone with Melody.

The mare stood at the back of her stall. Her chestnut coat was dull, and her frame looked thin compared to her bloated belly. She looked like she could use a good grooming and some supplements in her grain. She needed to be healthy to get through the last weeks of her pregnancy.

"And you need to learn to be less nervous," Amy said to her. "There's nothing to be scared of here."

Now that the others had left the doorway, Melody stepped cautiously forward. Her long forelock fell down over her broad, pretty face. She stretched her nose out toward Amy and blew softly down her nostrils.

Amy smiled and blew back, knowing that it was the mare's way of saying she wanted to be friends. Then, sliding the bolt on the door, she slipped quietly into the warm stall and waited for Melody to come right up to her. Amy stroked the mare's rough neck and smoothed her tangled forelock with her fingers. At first the mare was cautious, her muscles tense, but as Amy's fingers moved in small, light circles across her face and neck, she slowly began to relax.

Very gently, Amy moved so that she could place her hand on the taut, stretched skin of Melody's belly. She glanced at Melody's face, but the mare showed no sign of objecting so Amy let her hand rest there.

Somewhere, underneath her fingers, she knew, there was a foal. She shut her eyes and tried to imagine it. What would it be like? Was it OK? Or had it been injured by the accident? Was it still alive? She felt Melody's side rise and fall with every breath. *Be all right,* she urged, *please, please be all right.*

Although Amy wanted to stay with Melody all after-noon, she knew that the other horses needed attention, too, and after spending another half hour with the mare, she went outside and began to help Ben and Ty with the chores, stopping every now and then to check on Melody.

"We should probably try to protect the wound. I know she's on antibiotics, but it would be good to apply a salve to the outside of the cut as well," Ty said, joining Amy at Melody's door before feed time. "We'll have to be careful about what herbs we use because of her pregnancy, but garlic and kelp should both be safe. What do you think?"

Amy nodded. She knew that putting kelp in her feed would help improve the mare's skin and coat and that a garlic ointment should also help combat any infection that might come from her wound. At Heartland, they often treated the horses with herbs and other natural remedies. "Good idea. We could also add some Rescue Remedy to her water."

"Yeah," Ty agreed. "That should help her settle down and cope with the stress of being in a new place." He looked thoughtfully at the mare. "It might be better if you handle her over the next few days, Amy. She seems to have accepted you. While she's still recovering from the accident it would be good if she didn't have to deal with too many new people."

"I agree," Amy replied. She looked at the chestnut mare, happy to take sole charge of Melody for as long as necessary.

❧

After all the other horses had been fed and bedded down for the night and Ty and Ben had left, Amy went back to Melody's stall and began to gently groom her with a soft body brush. After an hour, the mare's coat was smoother and her mane and tail finally untangled, but Amy was still reluctant to leave her. What if something happened in the night? She sat down on an upturned bucket and watched the mare pulling peacefully at the pile of hay on the floor.

At eight o'clock, Grandpa came up to the stall. "Are you going to come in, honey?" he said, his hands buried deep in the pockets of his winter jacket. "It's getting late."

Amy looked around. "But what if she goes into labor?"

Grandpa's eyes swept over the mare. "She's not showing any signs of it." He took in Amy's reluctant face. "You can't sleep here every night until she has her foal," he said gently. "Leave her now, Amy. You can always come and check on her before you go to bed."

Knowing he was right, Amy stood up and stretched her stiff muscles. "See you later, girl," she said softly. Fastening the stall door, she followed her grandpa down to the farmhouse.

"Soraya called," he said as they reached the back door. "I told her you'd call her back."

"Thanks," Amy said, pulling off her boots. She had left a message on her best friend's answering machine that morning, telling her that a new horse was arriving. "Did you tell her about Melody's accident?"

"Only briefly," Jack replied. "I said you'd fill her in on all the details."

Going into the kitchen, Amy picked up the phone and headed up the stairs to her bedroom. "Don't be long,"

Jack called after her. "Supper will be ready in ten minutes."

"OK," Amy called back, starting to dial the number. She knew Soraya would be curious to know all about Melody and what had happened.

She was right. Soraya was bursting with questions. "What happened?" she demanded, as soon as she realized it was Amy. "Is the mare OK? Your grandpa said Scott was there and that he stitched her up. What about the foal?"

Amy sat cross-legged on her bed and explained everything.

"Scott thinks she's going to pull through, but she might still go into labor early, and we don't know if the foal's injured or not."

"Can I come and see her?" Soraya asked.

"Sure," Amy said. "Why don't you come over in the morning?"

"Great!" Soraya said. There was a tiny pause. "Will, er, Ben be around?" she said, her voice suddenly sounding deceptively casual.

Amy grinned. "Why?" she teased. "Aren't you coming over if he's not?"

"Of course I am!" Soraya exclaimed defensively. "I want to see Melody. It's just . . . well . . ."

"Relax," Amy broke in, laughing. "He'll be here. He already had his day off this week, and besides, even on his days off he seems to be here all the time. He's working really hard." She remembered about the High Prelim class. "Oh yeah, Ben's still taking Red to that show in two weeks, and he said we could both go with him to watch. But only if you want to, of course," she added.

"Want to?" Soraya yelled incredulously. "Try and stop me!"

Just then, Grandpa called up the stairs. "Amy! Dinner's ready!"

"I've got to go," Amy said to Soraya.

"I'll be over around ten tomorrow," her friend promised.

"OK," Amy said. "See you then!"

Chapter Three

❦

Amy had trouble sleeping that night. She had checked on Melody before she went to bed and the mare had been quiet, but she still couldn't help worrying. Her dreams were full of images of the mare lying on the grass, the bar of wood sticking out of her side.

Amy woke early and glanced at her alarm clock. *Five-thirty*. It was still dark outside, but she felt wide awake. Immediately, the events of the day before flashed in her head. She anxiously threw back the covers.

Her jeans and sweater were lying on the floor where she had left them the night before. Pulling them on, she crept down the quiet stairs and went into the kitchen. She *had* to see how Melody was. Taking the flashlight from the pine dresser, she went outside.

The air was frosty, but she hardly noticed as she ran

up the dark yard. She pulled back the barn doors and went inside. Hearing the noise, several of the other horses came to their stall doors in surprise. Amy hurried past them, her heart beating fast when she reached Melody's stall.

She shone the light over the door. Melody was dozing on her feet. However, as the light flashed past her head, Melody's eyes shot open and she started backward in alarm. Amy hastily angled the flashlight beam down to the floor.

"Easy, girl," she whispered, relief rushing through her as she realized Melody was OK. "It's only me."

She switched off the flashlight. Plunged into sudden blackness, it was a moment before her eyes started to adjust. Sliding back the bolts on Melody's door, Amy entered the warm stall. She could just make out the mare's shadowy outline.

"There's no need to be frightened," she said softly. She waited a moment and then heard the straw rustle as Melody turned and stepped cautiously toward her. Amy held out her hand and felt the mare's warm breath on her palm. With a quiet snort, the horse lifted her muzzle and blew gently, her breath flickering like soft fingertips across Amy's face.

For a long moment they stood there together cocooned in the darkness, Amy gently stroking the mare and the mare breathing in Amy's scent. Then, with a small sigh, Melody dropped her muzzle onto Amy's shoulder and let it rest there. It was the gesture of trust that Amy had been hoping for. She gently massaged the mare's neck with small clockwise circles.

"Poor girl," she whispered, feeling the weight of the horse's muzzle become heavier as she relaxed. "Your life's changed a lot recently, hasn't it? I guess you can't understand where your owner's gone or why you've been brought to this new place. But I'll look after you, I promise, and one day we'll find someone to love you just like Mrs. Phillips used to."

She leaned her face against the mare's cheek. It would be so much easier if horses could understand human language. The only way that she could show Melody what she meant was to treat her with respect and kindness and never do anything to break the trust the mare had placed in her.

✦

As the darkness outside slowly gave way to dawn, Amy stayed with Melody, massaging first her neck and shoulders and then her back, hindquarters, and legs. Gradually she felt the tension in the mare's muscles begin to seep away.

Engrossed in her work, the sound of the barn doors being pulled back at seven o'clock and the electric lights being switched on made her jump in surprise.

"Amy!" Ty said, seeing her look out over the stall door. "What are you doing?"

"I came to see Melody," Amy explained, yawning suddenly. "I didn't sleep too well last night."

Ty nodded understandingly and approached the stall. "How is she?"

"She seems fine," Amy said. "There's no sign of her going into labor. Her side's swollen and bruised, but I guess that's not surprising."

Ty rested his arms on top of the half-door. Melody, still not trusting anyone apart from Amy, shied to the back of the stall.

"It's all right, girl, Ty's not going to hurt you," Amy said, but the horse still looked wary.

Ty's eyes swept over her wound. "We could use some comfrey ointment. It should help reduce the bruising and speed up the healing process."

Amy nodded. "What do you think we should do about exercising her? We can't turn her out in the field. She might rip out her stitches if she rolls."

"We'll see what Scott says when he calls," Ty said.

They had just finished the feeding when Scott arrived. Amy held Melody while he examined her side. The mare flinched as the vet approached, but with Amy stroking and soothing her, she let Scott check her over. After the first few minutes, Amy felt her relax slightly.

"The wound's healing OK," Scott said as he finished

his examination, having given Melody a shot of antibiotics. "Just keep it clean, and make sure she doesn't rip her stitches."

"So how should we exercise her?" Amy asked, stroking Melody's dark muzzle.

"Walk her around on a lead rope," Scott replied, packing up his bag. "She needs to move her legs or they'll fill up with fluid, but don't turn her out. You might also want to get a foaling kit ready in a clean bucket with a lid."

"What goes in it?" Amy asked.

"Iodine, wound powder, cotton wool, a tail bandage, a towel, and a feeding bottle," Scott replied, going out of the stall. "I'll bring you some milk replacer tomorrow as well in case anything happens during the birth and the foal needs to be hand-fed. And it's probably a good idea to keep a bale of fresh straw and a pitchfork by her stall so you've got them on hand if she goes into labor unexpectedly."

"I'll get all that together," Amy said tentatively, following him out.

Scott saw the worry on her face. "She's doing fine, Amy," he said, gently. "It could have been a lot worse."

Amy looked into his reassuring eyes. "I just want her and the foal to be all right," she said, swallowing.

Scott gave her a pat on her shoulder. "We all want that," he said, looking at Melody still standing at the back of her stall, "but right now, there's nothing more we can do."

🙞

As Scott got into his Jeep to leave, Soraya's mom's car came up the drive and Amy ran to meet her friend.

"How's Melody?" Soraya asked, jumping out of the car.

"She's doing OK," Amy replied. "Getting better, Scott thinks." They both waved as the vet drove off.

"See you later, honey," Mrs. Martin, Soraya's mom, said, poking her head out of the car window. "I'll pick you up around four o'clock."

"'Bye, Mom!" Soraya called. She and Amy walked up the yard. "So where is she? Which stall is she in?"

"She's in the back barn," Amy said. "She's a bit nervous around people, though."

Just then, Ben came out of Jake's stall in the front stable block. "Hi, Soraya," he called. "Amy says you might come to watch me and Red at the show."

"Yeah," Soraya said, nodding eagerly. "If you're sure you don't mind."

"It'll be good to have the support," Ben said.

Soraya beamed.

"How about we all go out for a ride later?" Amy suggested, eager to get Soraya and Ben together as much as possible.

"That would be great!" Soraya exclaimed.

Ben nodded, too.

"We should see if Ty wants to come as well," Amy said to Soraya.

Ty was mucking out a stall in the back barn. "I'll pass," he said when Amy suggested a trail ride. "I'll stay and work Dancer in the ring."

"Are you sure?" Amy said, not wanting him to think they were all deserting him.

Ty nodded. "Yeah. Anyway, one of us should stay and keep an eye on Melody."

"Is this Melody?" Soraya asked, looking over a stall door.

"Yes, that's her." Amy said as she joined her friend. The chestnut mare had backed off from Soraya, but she pricked her ears as Amy let herself into the stall.

"She's lovely," Soraya said.

Melody snuffled at Amy's pockets. "I don't have anything for you," Amy told her.

"Here," Soraya offered, holding out some apple slices she had brought.

Amy took two slices and fed them to the mare, who greedily gobbled them up. "See if she'll take one from you," Amy suggested to Soraya. "She's got to start getting used to other people."

Soraya held out an apple. Melody stretched her head

forward hesitantly. "It's OK," Soraya murmured. "I won't hurt you."

The mare stepped forward and quickly took the treat. Then she stepped back, crunching the fruit. Soraya offered her another. This time, Melody took a more confident step forward. She ate the slice and then nudged Soraya's hand for more.

"Come on, let's leave her alone now," Amy said, pleased that the mare was showing signs of accepting Soraya. "We'll come back later and take her for a walk together."

They moved quietly out of the stall.

"Scott said to get a foaling kit ready," Amy said. "Will you give me a hand getting stuff together?"

"Sure," Soraya replied. "What do we need?"

Amy explained as they went down to the tack room to collect the equipment that Scott had suggested.

"Let's keep it all together in a bucket with a lid," Amy said, "so everything stays clean."

Just then, the phone rang in the house.

"I'll get that," Amy said, knowing her grandpa had gone out shopping. She ran down the yard, but by the time she had reached the kitchen Lou had already picked up the receiver.

"It's Judy Stillman, Ben's mom," Lou said as Amy opened the kitchen door. "Can you get him for me?"

Amy went outside. "Ben!" she yelled. "Phone!"

Ben came down the yard. "Who is it?" he asked.

"Your mom," Amy replied.

Ben stopped dead. "Can you tell her I'm not here?"

Amy frowned in surprise. "But she wants to talk with you."

"Well, I don't want to talk with her," Ben said. He turned abruptly and headed back up the yard.

Amy ran after him. "Ben! Wait up! You shouldn't just ignore your mom like this."

"Watch me," Ben said, going into Red's stall and sliding the door shut in Amy's face.

Amy stopped. What could she do? She couldn't drag Ben to the phone and make him speak to his mom. She hesitated and then headed back to the house. Lou had left the receiver on the table and was busily typing away at her laptop. "Where's Ben?" she said, looking up.

Amy shook her head and picked up the phone.

"Um, hi, Mrs. Stillman," she said. "It's Amy here. Ben can't, er, come to the phone right now. He's busy."

"What you're trying to say is that he's avoiding me," Judy Stillman said astutely.

"No, it's not that. He's just, um, just —" Amy stuttered uncertainly.

"It's OK," Ben's mom said quietly. "You don't have to make excuses for him. I've been leaving messages on his answering machine all week and he hasn't called me back." She paused. "I don't suppose *you* know what's going on, do you, Amy?"

Amy felt awkward. She didn't want to interfere. "Well, I think he was kind of looking forward to seeing you at the show," she admitted.

"That horse show!" Judy Stillman sounded surprised. "I didn't realize it meant that much to him. He acts like I'd be in the way if I were there."

"Well, he's probably just nervous. It's a big show for him." Amy said. "It's Red's first time competing at High Prelim level."

"Well, thanks for letting me know," Mrs. Stillman said. "Look, would you please ask him to call me soon?"

"No problem," Amy said. She replaced the phone in its cradle.

"What was that about?" Lou asked. "Why didn't Ben take the call?"

Before Amy could answer, the back door opened and Grandpa walked in with a box of groceries. "Hi, there," he said. Putting the box down, he reached into his jacket. "There's some mail for you," he said to Lou, taking out a handful of envelopes from his pocket. "There's one from England."

"From England!" The words burst from Lou, distracting her from the topic of Ben.

Amy looked at her sister in surprise.

Grandpa also noticed Lou's reaction. "Were you expecting something in particular?" he asked.

"Yes." Lou's cheeks flushed as she saw their curious glances. "But . . . but it's nothing important," she added quickly.

Despite her words, when Grandpa held the letter out, she grabbed it quickly, her eyes scanning the writing on the front. Flipping it over, she read the sender's address on the back. "Oh," she said, her face falling suddenly.

"Not what you were expecting?" Jack inquired.

Lou shook her head. "It's from Joanna, a friend of mine from boarding school." Looking up, she seemed to make an effort to smile. "I haven't heard from her for ages. What a nice surprise."

Amy frowned. Try as she might to hide it, Lou was obviously disappointed. What *had* she been expecting?

She couldn't forget her sister's expression, and going back to the tack room she told Soraya about it. "As soon as she heard there was a letter from England, she acted kind of strange," she said. "Like she thought it was something important."

"Like what?" Soraya asked.

"I don't know," Amy said. Lou had lots of friends in England. After their father had left, their mom had decided to return to Virginia to live with Jack at her childhood home. She had taken Amy with her, but Lou, age eleven, had begged to be allowed to stay on at her English boarding school. "It didn't seem like it was just a letter she was expecting from a friend," Amy said. "It seemed like she was *really* waiting for something to arrive."

"Maybe she's applied for a job over in England," Soraya suggested.

"She couldn't have!" Amy said. "She's decided to stay here."

Before their mom's death, Lou had been working in Manhattan, and although for a while it had looked as if she was going to return to her city life, she had eventually changed her mind and announced that she would stay at Heartland.

Soraya nodded. "Yeah. After all, she'd have told you if she was thinking of leaving. And anyway, things seem to be going really well with her and Scott. It's probably something else."

Amy hoped Soraya was right. After spending most of her childhood apart from Lou, she hated the thought of her sister going to live abroad just as they were beginning to really get to know each other. She nodded. "But what could it be?"

Soraya shrugged. "Why don't you ask her?"

Amy looked doubtful. She recalled the way that Lou

had reacted when Grandpa had asked her about the letter. It was apparent that she had a secret and she wasn't about to tell anyone what it was.

Soraya saw the concern on Amy's face. "Look," she said, practically. "If it's really important you'll find out sooner or later. There's no point worrying about it now."

Amy sighed. She guessed Soraya was right, but she hated the thought of Lou keeping secrets. After everything that had happened over the past six months, she just wanted life to be uncomplicated for a while.

"Come on," her friend said, linking arms with her. "Let's go see Melody again and take her for that walk."

Chapter Four

On the way to Melody's stall, Amy saw Ben going into the feed room with a pile of empty haynets. She remembered the message from his mother.

"Ben! Your mom asked if you'd give her a call back," she told him.

Ben nodded curtly and walked on.

Amy hesitated for a second and then followed. After her conversation with Judy Stillman, she was convinced that Ben's mom really wasn't as bad as he made her out to be. "She sounded worried that you hadn't returned her calls," she said.

Ben swung around. "So?" he said. "What do I care?"

Amy tried to keep calm. "Look, why don't you just call her? Is it really that big a deal?"

"I'll do what I want! OK? She's my mom, and I'll deal

with her," Ben said furiously. He threw the haynets on the pile and brushed by her as he headed out the door.

Amy was just about to go after him when Soraya reached her. "What's going on?" she asked.

Amy sighed. "Ben won't talk to his mom." She quickly told Soraya what had happened.

To her surprise, Soraya frowned. "Actually, Amy," she said, "Ben's got a point. It is *his* problem, not yours."

Amy glared at her, but Soraya met her gaze calmly. "You think I'm interfering?" she said more quietly, feeling her temper begin to die down.

Soraya nodded.

"I just get so frustrated," Amy said emotionally. "You know, when I think about what happened to Mom and how I would do anything to have her here still . . ." Her voice trailed off.

Soraya squeezed her arm. "I know," she said. "But you can't tell him what to do. He has to figure it out himself."

Amy looked at her. "I guess," she said, her voice almost a whisper. "I guess you're right."

❧

Later that morning, Amy, Ben, and Soraya tacked up for their ride.

"Where should we go?" Soraya asked as they mounted.

She seemed determined to be extra cheerful to make up for the tension that was still lingering between Amy and Ben.

"How 'bout to Pine Ridge," Amy suggested. "There are some great open fields for cantering over there and logs to jump." She had decided to ride Gypsy, thinking that it would be a chance to take the mare out for a good long workout to see if she showed any hints of bucking again.

"Oh, good!" Soraya said enthusiastically. She patted Moochie, the big bay hunter she was riding. He had been found neglected in a tiny paddock several months earlier and had come to Heartland to be nursed back to health. He was sturdy and strong again and was ready to be rehomed.

They let the horses trot along the trail that led across to Pine Ridge, the trees shielding them from the worst of the wind. As they rode, Amy felt her frustration with Ben's situation drain away.

He seemed more relaxed, too. Seeing a couple of fallen logs at the side of the trail, he turned in his saddle. "Want to jump these?" he called.

"OK," Amy said. "I'll go first."

She clicked her tongue and cantered Gypsy toward the two logs. The mare jumped them without a problem and pulled up calmly on the other side. "Good girl," Amy praised, patting her and turning to watch the others.

Moochie cleared the logs easily. Soraya pulled up alongside Amy, and together they watched Ben. Seeing the other two horses jump had excited Red. He flung his head up and plunged forward. Red was taking short, agitated steps and pulling at the reins. Amy watched cautiously to see what Ben would do. At one time, she knew he would have seen the horse's behavior as a challenge, a battle that had to be won no matter how wound up the horse became. But now he trotted Red past the logs, patting the horse's neck as he veered away from the jumps.

"Aren't you going to jump them?" Soraya said as he trotted toward them.

"Yes," Ben said. "But not until he's calm."

He steered Red away from them in a large circle. The chestnut visibly started to relax, his head and neck lowering as he listened to Ben's directions. Gathering the reins up slightly, Ben turned him toward the logs. Calm now, Red kept an even stride and jumped both smoothly, his ears pricked.

"That was really good," Amy burst out as Ben cantered up to them. Amy was relieved that Ben was becoming a more patient rider. Red really seemed to be responding to Ben's new training methods — the same methods that Heartland endorsed, building a bond of trust and understanding between horse and rider.

"Red's a beautiful jumper," Soraya commented as they all continued along the trail.

"I know. He's getting better all the time," Ben said, stroking the chestnut's shoulder. "I'm lucky."

"You can't give him all the credit. He really responds well to you," Amy said.

Ben shrugged. "I tell you, it's all Red. He'd jump with a three-year-old on his back."

Amy knew it wasn't true. Although Red was very talented at jumping, he was also pretty sensitive and needed a rider as good as Ben to bring out the best in him. "I guarantee he wouldn't go as well for another rider," she persisted.

Ben flushed slightly and shortened his reins. "Come on," he said, looking like he wanted to change the subject. "Let's canter."

They stayed out on the trails for almost two hours. Gypsy didn't show any signs of bucking, but when Soraya asked if she could go back to her owners soon, Amy shook her head.

"She still doesn't seem quite ready," she said. She glanced at the mare's arched neck. Maybe it was the way Gypsy's muscles tensed when she was excited, or the way she snaked her head down to free the reins whenever she felt her rider relax. Whatever the reason, Amy instinctively felt that she couldn't completely trust the black mare.

When Amy, Ben, and Soraya got back to Heartland, they turned the three horses out in the field and helped Ty finish off the remaining barn chores.

Soraya had to leave at four o'clock, but Ty and Ben stayed until all the horses had been fed and stabled and the yard swept.

"See you tomorrow!" Amy called as the guys finally got into their pickups to go home.

"Night!" Ty shouted back. "Don't stay up too late with Melody."

Amy grinned. Sometimes Ty seemed to know her too well!

She waved them off and then, collecting a grooming bucket from the tack room, went up to Melody's stall. The mare was looking over her door. She pricked her ears when she saw Amy and, for the first time since she had arrived at Heartland, whinnied a greeting.

"Hi, Melody," Amy said, delighted that the mare seemed so pleased to see her.

She stroked Melody's nose, then tied her up and began the grooming. As she brushed and curried, Amy let her mind go blank. She didn't think about Lou and the mystery letter she was waiting for, she didn't think about Ben and his problems, she just concentrated on rhythmically sweeping the brush across Melody's dull coat until a faint shine began to emerge.

At last she paused and wiped the back of one hand

across her hot, dusty forehead. "You're a good girl," she murmured. "I'll call Mr. Phillips tonight and tell him how you're doing."

She pulled the brush across the currycomb to clean its bristles of dirt and grease. But as she stepped toward Melody again, she froze. The mare's side seemed to jerk. Amy stared. There! It happened again! A definite movement!

Amy's heart somersaulted. Dropping the brush, she put her hand against Melody's side. This time she felt as well as saw it. A kicking movement! A kick so strong that the shape of a small hoof could almost be seen through Melody's coat. It was the foal! It must be alive!

"Oh, Melody," Amy whispered in delight.

Melody snorted softly. She seemed completely unconcerned about the kicking. Undoing her halter, Amy quickly kissed her nose and ran out of the stall. She had to tell Grandpa and Lou!

She raced down the yard, her heart banging. It was the first sign they'd had that the foal was alive. She couldn't wait to share the news.

Kicking off her boots, she ran into the house. A casserole was bubbling on the kitchen stove, but the kitchen was empty. Suddenly, Amy heard Lou and Grandpa talking in the hall. She hurried toward the connecting door, but as she reached it, her grandpa's words stopped her in her tracks.

"And you haven't told Amy?"

Amy paused, her hand hovering over the door handle. *Told me what?* she thought.

She heard her sister's voice. "Only Scott knows. I didn't want to say anything until I got a reply, Grandpa. I didn't want to get Amy's hopes up. It's been so awful waiting, knowing that each day there could be a letter."

A letter! Amy felt her spine tingle. They must be talking about the letter Lou was expecting from England. *But what's it got to do with me?* she wondered.

"Lou, you have to tell her," Grandpa said, and Amy noticed an intensity in his voice that she had never heard before. "You should have told her before you wrote in the first place."

"But what if he doesn't write back?" Lou said.

"Amy still has the right to know. You can't —"

It was too much. "I've got the right to know what?" Amy said, opening the door.

Grandpa and Lou swung around.

"Amy!" Lou exclaimed, shocked.

"How long have you been there?" Grandpa said quickly.

Amy didn't answer him. She was staring at Lou. "What should you have told me, Lou?" she demanded.

Lou looked desperately at Grandpa. "I — well —" she stammered.

"What is it?" Amy cried, feeling increasingly alarmed. "Lou? *Who* did you write to?"

Look took a breath. "Daddy," she said.

For a moment, Amy was too shocked to speak. *Daddy?* She stared at Lou. Somehow she knew that was the answer, but she was still caught off guard.

"I wrote to him after we found the letter in Mom's room." The words came out of Lou in a rush. "I sent it to the address on the back of the envelope in the hope that he still lives there. I told him about Mom and that — we wanted to see him."

"*See* him!" Amy exclaimed, finding her voice at last. She stepped backward. "Are you kidding?"

She felt as if her world were falling down around her. All her life, her father had been a distant, shadowy figure. Sure, she had sometimes felt curious about him, wondered what he looked like, whether she was like him, but she had never wanted to *meet* him. He had abandoned them, and although she could not remember him, she could remember the nights when her mom had cried as if she were never going to stop, when nothing and no one had been able to comfort her. Mom had recovered in the end, moved on, founded Heartland. But Amy had always known that the sadness from that time had never left her; it had just been pushed way under the surface.

She shook her head. "I don't want to see him! I won't!"

"But he's our father!" Lou exclaimed.

"So?" Amy cried. "He abandoned us!"

"He tried to make things right!" Lou protested. "You saw the letter, Amy. He wanted to get back together with Mom. He wanted to be with us again."

"I don't care!" Amy shouted.

"Amy, calm down," Jack Bartlett said, stepping toward her. "We don't even know if he got the letter. It's been five years since he wrote to your mom. That address is probably old."

Amy looked at him desperately. "But what if it isn't?" she exclaimed. "Grandpa, what if he writes back and wants to come here?" Her eyes frantically searched his face. Surely Grandpa didn't want Daddy to come to Heartland. "Think of what he did to Mom — to us!"

A shadow crossed Jack's eyes. "I . . ." His voice trailed off and in that moment, in the look she saw cross his face, Amy knew she was right.

Lou must also have seen the expression in their grandpa's eyes. "Grandpa!" she exclaimed, horrified.

"Lou —" Jack began, but then he broke off, shaking his head. "Look, let's not argue, we can discuss it more when — *if* — he writes back."

"He will!" Lou said defensively. "I know he will!"

"Honey, don't get your hopes up too high," Jack said wearily. "After all, he's always known the address here, and even if your mom hadn't wanted to see him, he could have gotten in touch with you at any time."

"But maybe he was worried about how Mom would react," Lou said. "Now he has my letter and he *knows* that we want to see him."

Amy felt indignant. "*You* want to," she said. "Don't go making promises for me, Lou. As far as I'm concerned, I don't have a father anymore."

Lou turned on her, her eyes flashing with exasperation. "Amy!"

"No more arguing!" Jack held up his hands and looked at them both. *"Please."*

Amy saw the tension around his mouth and eyes and bit back the angry words that were springing to her lips. It couldn't be easy for Grandpa. He had always tried to be neutral about their father when he came up in conversation, but now she realized how hard this must have been for him. He'd been the one who had helped their mom slowly piece her life back together after the breakup. Arguing with Lou would only upset him even more.

She stared mutinously at her sister but didn't say another word.

"Thank you," Jack said quietly. "Now, can we just agree to deal with this later?"

Amy and Lou stared at each other, the silence between them weighted with anger. But Lou seemed as reluctant as Amy to upset Grandpa further. She nodded. "OK," she said.

Amy nodded, too, and saw the relief on Grandpa's face. "I'm going to get changed," she muttered, heading for the staircase. Right now, she just wanted to be alone.

In her room, she sat down on the bed. Her thoughts were whirling, and it was only now that she remembered she had meant to tell Grandpa and Lou about Melody's foal kicking. Right this moment, even *that* didn't seem important. How *could* Lou have just written to their father without discussing it with her first?

But then, deep inside, Amy knew. Her mom had often told her about the special bond that Lou and Daddy had shared. She had said how similar they were — both practical, brave, determined. Amy had seen the photographs that her mom had kept of the two of them riding together. She couldn't imagine how Lou felt at eleven, when Daddy abandoned them.

Thinking about the photographs, Amy opened her bedside drawer and rooted around until she found a photo that she kept in there. It was one of all four of them — her, Lou, Mom, and Daddy — sitting on a beach beside an enormous sand castle. They were all smiling. She looked at herself, a skinny two-year-old with straight dark blond hair, standing by Mom. Daddy had his arm around Lou's shoulders.

Amy studied her father's features and then took the photograph over to the mirror. She looked more like him than her mom. They had the same thickly lashed gray eyes, the same high, wide cheekbones and determined mouths. And yet she didn't know him at all. They shared the same features, but they were strangers.

She looked at the photograph again. "I don't want to see you," she whispered.

Despite her words, Amy knew that deep down inside, in a hidden corner of her heart, she desperately longed to know what her father was like.

Chapter Five

When Amy opened her eyes the next morning, she lay in bed for a moment with the feeling that she had just woken from a horrible dream. Then everything came flooding back. It wasn't a dream; it was real. Lou had written to Daddy. He might write back. He might even want to come and visit.

Well, I won't be here, Amy thought, hurriedly pushing back the covers and getting out of bed. *I'll go stay with Soraya. I'm not seeing him. I don't care what Lou says.*

She got dressed quickly, wanting to get out of the house before either Lou or Grandpa got up. Dinner, the night before, had been strained. She and Lou had hardly spoken a word to each other, and Grandpa had been quiet, lost in his own thoughts.

As Amy got the morning feeds ready, she heard the

sound of a car driving up outside the house. She looked out of the feed room and saw Ben getting out of his sporty black pickup. "You're early," she called in surprise. She glanced at her watch. It was only six-thirty, an hour before Ben officially started work.

Ben shrugged. "It's always more of a rush to get things done the days you're at school. I knew it would help if I got started now."

He was right, but even so, Amy didn't want him to feel obliged to have such long days. "We can manage," she said, seeing shadows of tiredness under his eyes. "You don't have to put in all these extra hours."

"It's no problem," Ben said, coming into the feed room. "What should I do? The haynets?"

Amy gave a shrug and nodded. There was no point arguing. If he wanted to work so hard, she wasn't going to stop him.

Ben picked up the pile of empty nets and took them to the small hay storage bin that had been built on to the stone feed room. Every few days the hay bin was filled up with bales from the big barn behind the tack room. Grandpa had built it so that the full haynets didn't have to be lugged all the way from the barn twice a day. Amy heard the sound of Ben shaking out the compact flakes of hay. "How's Melody this morning?" he called.

With a start, Amy stopped mixing up the feeds. She had almost forgotten the news about the foal! She rushed around to the hay bin. "Her foal's definitely alive!" she said. She quickly told Ben all about seeing and feeling the kicking movement in Melody's side.

"That's great," Ben said, straightening up immediately. "They normally start kicking a couple of weeks before they're born. Jack and Lou must be relieved."

Amy hesitated. "They don't know yet," she admitted.

Ben looked at her in astonishment. "You haven't told them?"

Amy shook her head. "Things were weird last night. We had a bit of an argument," she said, realizing that she needed to give him some sort of explanation. "I just wasn't in the mood to deal with it." She didn't want to say any more and she turned hastily. "I'll go give the horses their feeds," she said, and grabbing a pile of feed buckets, she strode out into the yard.

❧

To Amy's relief, Ben didn't ask for any more details. They fed and watered the horses and then, leaving him to start on the stalls, Amy went inside to get ready for school.

Coming downstairs after taking a shower, she found Lou sitting at the kitchen table reading the paper over a cup of coffee. Hearing the sound of her footsteps, Lou looked up, but then seeing it was Amy, she immediately looked down again.

Ignoring her sister, Amy got a bowl and poured out

some cereal. She sat down at the far end of the table and ate it quickly.

Just as Amy was finishing, Grandpa came into the kitchen. "Morning," he said. The two girls looked up.

"Hi, Grandpa," Amy said, getting up and putting her empty bowl in the sink. "Do you want some coffee?"

Jack nodded. "Thanks."

Amy poured him a cup and was just about to tell him about Melody's foal when the back door burst open. Ty stood in the porch. "Ben just told me about Melody's foal!" he said, looking delighted. "It's great!"

Amy saw Grandpa and Lou look at Ty in confusion. "What?" Grandpa said blankly.

"About the foal kicking!" Ty said in surprise. He turned quickly to Amy, a frown crossing his face. "Ben said you saw it last night."

Amy felt herself start to go red. "Yeah, I did," she admitted.

"Well, that's wonderful!" Lou exclaimed, getting to her feet. "It must be a real survivor after that fall."

"Why didn't you tell us?" Grandpa said to Amy.

"I was just about to," Amy said. She grabbed her backpack off the floor, not wanting to bring up the tension of the night before by explaining. "I'm going to school," she said, turning away from Lou's and Jack's astonished expressions.

"Amy —" Grandpa began, but Amy didn't stop.

"I'll be late. See you this afternoon," she said as she ran out of the house.

Ty followed her. "Hey, what's going on?" he asked, catching up with her.

Amy paused for a moment. "It's a long story," she said, her eyes begging him not to question her. "I'll — I'll tell you tonight." Shifting her backpack onto her shoulder, she set off down the drive.

"See you later," Ty called.

Amy nodded but didn't look back. She knew she'd have to explain things to him later, but right this minute she didn't feel like talking about it — not to Ty, not even to Soraya.

"You're quiet today," Soraya said, when the bus reached school. "Are you OK?"

"Yeah, fine," Amy said quickly.

Soraya didn't look convinced. "Are you sure?"

"Yes!" Amy insisted.

Soraya held her gaze for a moment but then, to Amy's relief, seemed to decide not to press the matter further.

Amy couldn't concentrate at all that day. Every time a teacher started talking, she drifted off into her own thoughts. Had the mail arrived at home? Maybe even now Lou was opening a letter from their father.

Maybe, somewhere in England, he was reading Lou's letter, or at this moment he was sitting down and writing a reply.

Amy could tell that Soraya knew something was up. Being best friends since third grade, they knew each other inside out. On the way home in the bus that afternoon, Amy finally gave up trying to pretend nothing was wrong and told her everything.

Soraya's eyes widened. "Lou wrote to your dad!" She spoke in a low voice so that no one else could hear, but her face showed her shock. "When?"

"About six weeks ago," Amy said. "She's been waiting to hear back."

Soraya's eyes scanned Amy's face. "What are you going to do if he gets in touch with you?"

"I don't know," Amy said, pushing a hand through her hair. "Lou wants to see him, of course, but . . ." Her voice trailed off.

"You don't?" Soraya said, finishing the thought for her.

Amy saw the understanding in her friend's dark brown eyes. "No," she said, shaking her head. "I don't *ever* want to see him." She spoke the words as if trying to convince herself that what she was saying was true.

"What about your grandpa?" Soraya asked. "What'd he say?"

"That we should wait and see if he gets in touch," Amy

replied. She remembered the look that had crossed his face the night before. "No matter what he says, I *know* he doesn't want Daddy at Heartland." Her voice rose slightly. "I just don't get how Lou can be so selfish! She must know that Grandpa wouldn't want to see him. I mean, he was the one who had to look after Mom after my father left us. What was Lou thinking?" she demanded.

Soraya hesitated. "Well, I guess she misses your dad. She probably still loves him."

"How can she?" Amy exploded. Suddenly realizing that several kids nearby had turned to look at them both, she dropped her voice again. "I hate him," she hissed. The back of her eyes felt hot. "I'll never forgive him for what he did to Mom. *I can't!*" Her eyes blurred and she looked quickly down at her knees and angrily blinked back her tears.

Soraya reached out and squeezed her hand.

Amy continued to stare at her knees. *I mean it,* she thought. *I hate him, and I'll never forgive him!*

When Amy got off the school bus she went straight to Melody's stall. She wanted to push all thoughts about her father to the back of her mind. "Hello, girl," she murmured as Melody gave a welcoming nicker. "Did you miss me?"

Melody nuzzled her shoulder in reply.

"She seems to be settling down a bit."

Amy turned when she heard the voice. It was Ty.

"I've been in with her a few times today," he said. "And I think she's beginning to get used to me." He came over to the door and offered his palm for Melody to sniff. The mare cautiously stretched her muzzle forward and blew in and out.

"That's a big improvement," Amy said. "A few days ago she wouldn't have come anywhere near you."

"We could take her out for a walk together," Ty suggested.

Amy smiled. "I'll just get changed."

She ran down to the house and quickly pulled on her old jeans and sweater.

"Let's walk down the drive," Amy said, joining Ty in Melody's stall.

At first, Melody's ears flickered backward uneasily, and she kept looking at Ty warily as he walked beside Amy down the drive, but after a few minutes, she began to relax.

"Have you called Mr. Phillips yet to tell him how she's doing?" Ty asked Amy as they stopped to let her graze for a few moments.

Amy shook her head, remembering that she had been going to. "I will. I was going to last night, but then" — she hesitated — "well . . . something happened."

She saw Ty's curious look and knew that she couldn't

keep it from him any longer. When she had finished relating the events of the previous evening, his reaction was much the same as Soraya's — concerned understanding.

"It must have been a real shock for you," he said.

"It was," Amy admitted. "But I'm not going to see him." She spoke the words more confidently than she had on the bus. The more she said them, the more she felt herself believing in them.

Ty nodded. "I can understand why."

"Lou doesn't," Amy said quietly.

Ty looked at her sympathetically. "It'll be OK," he said. "You'll see."

Amy wished she could believe him. Just the thought of Daddy coming back caused a wave of panic to well up inside her. She looked quickly at Melody and changed the subject. "Here, you hold her," she said, handing Ty the lead rope.

Ty took it and moved closer. Melody side-stepped away from him. "Easy, girl," he murmured.

Melody glanced at him suspiciously for a moment, but then she relaxed and began to crop at the short winter grass again. Ty reached out and gently stroked the mare's neck. She didn't flinch or move away.

"She's starting to like you," Amy said softly.

Ty nodded. "We'll get there in the end," he replied. "We just have to take things slowly for a while."

❧

They had just put Melody back in her stall when Ben came into the barn. "Hi," he said, seeing Amy. "So, did Ty tell you about our mystery visitor?"

"Mystery visitor?" Amy echoed.

"Oh, it was just this guy who came up to the house," Ty said dismissively. "Your grandpa said he was looking for work."

"He kind of hung around after Jack talked with him, though," Ben said. "And before he left, he looked in all the stalls. I think he was a reporter."

"Yeah, right." Amy couldn't help smiling. "Why wouldn't he have said he was a reporter, then?"

"You never know," Ben said. "Maybe it's something undercover."

Ty grinned at Amy. "He's been going on about it all day. He was just some guy looking for work. Word is probably getting around that business has picked up for us." He shut Melody's door. "Ivy, Solo, and Sundance need riding. We could take them out on the trails."

Amy ran down to the house to get her hard hat. Grandpa and Lou were in the kitchen.

"Hi," Amy said, grabbing her hat from the easy chair by the TV.

Lou didn't say anything. She just went on looking

through the barn records, but Grandpa smiled and looked up from the catalog he was reading. "Hi, honey."

"I'm just going out for a ride with Ty and Ben," Amy said. As she reached the door, she remembered the conversation in the barn. "Oh, Ben and Ty were talking about the guy who came by today."

To her surprise, Grandpa started violently in his chair.

"A man?" Lou said, looking up curiously.

The shocked expression on Jack Bartlett's face quickly smoothed out. "It was just someone looking for casual work," he said, his voice light. "You were out, Lou. It was no big deal."

"Ben seems to think it was." Amy grinned. "He's convinced he was an undercover reporter. Maybe it was a spy sent by Greenbriar," Amy offered with a laugh. Greenbriar was a rival stable across town.

Lou shook her head and turned back to the records. But when Amy glanced at Grandpa, his face looked taut with distress. "Are you OK, Grandpa?" she asked in concern.

"Me?" Jack said in surprise.

"Yeah, you don't look like yourself," Amy said.

Jack looked down at the catalog again. "I'm just a little tired. Old age catching up with me, that's all." He smiled at her but she noticed that his eyes looked distracted. "I'm fine, just fine."

Amy smiled back, but she couldn't help feeling

slightly concerned. Grandpa was very fit and healthy, and although he was sixty-eight years old now, he hardly ever showed any signs of old age. Hoping that he was telling the truth, Amy went back outside.

✍

Over the next few days, Amy continued to notice that Grandpa didn't seem to be his usual self. Quieter than normal, he seemed to be lost in thought. She was consumed with thought as well, wondering what the day's mail would bring. But by Friday, there was still no response to Lou's letter.

"Oh, Melody." Amy sighed as she groomed the mare on Friday night. "What's going to happen?"

Amy stroked the mare's smooth neck. With good food and daily grooming sessions, the mare's chestnut coat was at last beginning to shine and her skin had lost its dryness. The hollows in her flanks had begun to fill out, and most important of all to Amy, the wariness had left her eyes. "You're going to have the most beautiful foal," she said, watching Melody's side twitch with a sudden kick. "And it'll go out in the fields with you and graze on the grass and gallop at your side. Won't that be wonderful?"

There was a noise at the stall door and Amy swung around. Ty was standing there, car keys in hand. "One day I'm going to put a tape recorder in here," he said with a grin. "It would make very interesting listening."

"You talk to the horses, too," Amy protested.

"I don't have complete conversations with them," Ty teased. He shook his head. "Well, I'm off. I'll see you tomorrow. I was thinking of going to the cemetery to visit your mom's grave at lunchtime. Do you want to come?"

"I'd like that," Amy said. She tried to go to the cemetery as often as possible, but with the darker evenings and the winter chores it was getting more difficult to find time to visit.

"I'll get some flowers," Ty said.

Amy nodded. "See you tomorrow, then."

"Yeah, later," Ty said, and he left.

❧

The next day at lunchtime, Amy and Ty got into his battered pickup and set off for the cemetery.

"I'm glad you asked me. I haven't been over there for a few weeks," Amy said. "We've been so busy. I was going to go last weekend but then Melody arrived." She paused. "I wonder what Mom would have done with Melody." She often found herself wondering how her mom would have treated the new horses that came to them. She knew that she had to rely on her own intuition and knowledge, but it was hard not to wonder whether Mom would have done things differently.

Ty looked at her reassuringly. "Probably exactly what

we've done. Melody's wound's healing well; she's looking good. And she's a lot quieter. You've done a great job."

"I guess," Amy said, feeling a bit happier. "I just hope that the birth goes without a hitch. Now that we know the foal's alive, I hope it's healthy."

Ty nodded and they drove on in silence.

Finally, they reached the cemetery parking lot and got out. Tall trees loomed overhead, their bare branches outlined against the dull, gray sky. It was a cold, frosty day, and as they walked down the path toward Marion's grave, their breath froze like white smoke in the air.

"I wonder when we'll get the first snow," Ty said as their boots crunched on the stone path.

Amy nodded. When it snowed, the workload at Heartland increased, the water troughs froze, the yard became icy, and the ground in the schooling rings became hard, so there was less chance to exercise the horses. She dug her hands in her pockets and hoped that the snow would hold off for a while longer.

They rounded the corner that led to the quiet area of the cemetery where Marion was buried. Suddenly, Amy stopped. "Hey, is that man at Mom's grave?" she questioned.

A man was kneeling about thirty feet away, his head bowed. Hearing her voice, he looked around and rose swiftly to his feet. He was tall, with slightly graying hair.

He looked like he'd once been handsome, but now deep lines were etched across his face.

A swift rush of anger rose inside Amy. What was he doing? "Who are you?" Amy said under her breath. Then, as the curiosity swelled inside her, she repeated the question with more force. She began to stride down the path toward him. "What are you doing? This is my mom's grave."

The man stared at her as she approached, and for a moment, she thought he was going to speak. But then a strange, haunted look crossed his eyes, and he suddenly turned and cut across the grass to the far path.

Amy stopped and stared after the figure, noticing as he hurried away that he had a slight limp. She swung around to Ty. "What was that about?" she demanded indignantly.

Ty was frowning. He had an incredulous look on his face.

"What is it?" Amy said.

"I know this sounds odd, but that is the guy who came by Heartland the other day looking for work," Ty replied. "I'm sure of it."

Amy stared at him. "What was he doing here?"

"I don't know," Ty said, sounding mystified. "Maybe he *is* a reporter," he added, trying to break the tension.

Amy looked for the man, but he had vanished into the mist.

❧

"He was kneeling right next to Mom's grave!" Amy told Grandpa and Lou when she arrived back at Heartland, half an hour later. "I went over to talk to him, but he just ran away."

The two of them had been eating lunch, and now Lou put down her knife and fork. "And Ty said it was the same man who came by the other day?"

"He says he's sure of it," Amy said anxiously. Now that her initial shock had passed, she felt angry. She didn't like the idea of some strange guy hanging around her mom's grave. It was creepy and weird.

Lou frowned and turned to Grandpa. "Did this guy say anything about knowing Mom when he was here?"

For a moment, Jack looked like he was about to shake his head, but then he seemed to stop himself, and for the first time, Amy noticed that the muscles in his face were tense. A red tinge spread along his cheekbones.

"Grandpa, what is it?" Amy said, seeing his guarded expression.

But he didn't speak.

Amy's heart suddenly began to thump in her chest. There was something wrong — something dreadfully wrong.

"Grandpa?" Lou said, and from the high tone of her

voice Amy could tell that Grandpa's expression was unnerving her, too.

Jack cleared his throat. "There's . . . something you should know," he said. He looked at Amy. "The man you saw — the man who came around the other day — isn't a stranger. He's —" He took a deep breath. "He's your father."

Chapter Six

For a moment, the world stood still, and then the room and everything in it seemed to rush away from Amy at high speed. She clutched the back of the chair she was standing behind. "What?" she stammered in shock.

"That man is your father," Grandpa repeated.

"What do you mean?" Amy cried.

"No!" Lou gasped, almost at the same time.

Amy's gaze frantically scanned her grandpa's face, desperately looking for him to shake his head, to smile. But he didn't. His blue eyes were grave. "I should have told you right from the start," he said heavily. "I know it was wrong. When he came over, I told him that you didn't want to see him. I told him to leave."

"You did *what*?" Lou burst out, pushing her chair back violently.

Amy jumped. Through the shock of the announcement, she had almost forgotten about Lou. Now she saw that furious color was flooding her sister's cheeks.

"You told Daddy to go away?" Lou said, staring at Grandpa. "How *could* you?" she cried, her voice rising. "You know how much I want to see him!"

"Yes, I know," Jack said, sounding wretched. "But Lou, I had to." He stood up and stepped toward her. "I was the one who had to pick up the pieces after he left your mother. I saw how he almost destroyed her, Lou. I couldn't have him here."

He reached out for her, but Lou jerked her arm away. She stared at him. "You can't go on protecting her after she's gone. I wanted to see him. I need to see him. I'll never forgive you for this, Grandpa!" she spat, her eyes welling with tears. "Never!"

"Lou —" Amy said, going toward her.

"No! Leave me alone!" Lou cried. With a sob, she grabbed her car keys and ran out of the kitchen, slamming the back door.

"Lou!" Jack wailed. But by the time he and Amy had reached the doorway, Lou was already starting the engine of her car.

"What did I do?" Jack whispered as Lou drove off at high speed. He turned, his face pale.

Amy saw the despair in his eyes. "She'll be OK,

Grandpa," she said, desperately trying to ignore the frantic hammering of her heart. "She'll come back soon."

But by six o'clock that evening, Lou still hadn't come back. Amy had briefly explained to Ty what had happened, and after the horses had been fed, he had come down to the house to wait with her and Grandpa.

"It's been three hours now," Grandpa said, getting up and pacing across the floor. "Where is she?"

"Maybe she went to Scott's?" Ty suggested.

Grandpa picked up the phone and began to dial the vet's number.

Ty pressed Amy's hand. "You OK?" he asked.

Amy nodded numbly. Since her grandpa has made the announcement, her mind had gone into shock. Every so often an image of the man — her father — standing by the grave flashed into her mind, but each time she pushed it away. To think that she had actually seen him, spoken to him, and not recognized him was just too much to think about. But thinking about Lou wasn't any easier. Where had she gone? Was she all right?

She looked at Ty and saw the concern in his dark eyes. "Lou will be fine," he murmured, squeezing her hand again. "She just needs some time to cool off."

Amy swallowed and looked down. She desperately

wanted to believe him, but she couldn't help thinking the worst. What if Lou had been involved in an accident? It was almost dark outside and it had begun to rain — the roads would be wet and slippery. She fought back the fear that rose inside her as memories flashed into her mind, memories of a day five months ago when she and Mom had been driving through the rain. In her mind, she saw the sodden road, the sleeting rain, the trailer skidding toward the fallen tree. . . .

"Scott, it's Jack here."

The sound of her grandpa's voice jerked Amy from her nightmare thoughts. Her eyes scanned his face as he asked if Scott had seen Lou. There was a pause, and then seeing the hope die from his eyes, Amy knew what the answer had been.

"She left here more than three hours ago," she heard Grandpa say. "We had an argument. It's too difficult to explain over the phone, but she's upset — very upset."

He replaced the handset. "Scott's going to come over."

Just then, the back door opened and Ben came in. "I'm going home now, if that's OK," he said, stamping his feet on the mat. He looked around at their worried faces. "Is everything all right?"

Amy nodded. She had simply told him that there had been a family disagreement. "Yeah, you call it a day," she said, forcing herself to smile. "We'll be fine."

"You're sure there isn't anything I can do?" Ben asked.

Amy shook her head. "See you tomorrow."

" 'Bye, then," Ben said.

Scott arrived twenty minutes later. He came into the kitchen, shaking the raindrops off his jacket.

"So what happened exactly?" he said quickly.

As Jack explained, the concern on Scott's face deepened. "And she just took off without saying where she was going?"

Grandpa nodded. "I tried to stop her, but she wouldn't listen." He stood still by the sink and rubbed his face with his hands. "I should never have done what I did," he said to Scott with a sigh, "but when Tim just showed up, I couldn't stop myself. I know how he almost destroyed Marion, and I couldn't stand by and see him upset my granddaughters." He looked wretchedly at Amy. "Please try to understand, honey, I was just trying to protect you — to protect us all."

Amy hated seeing the guilt on his face. "I know, Grandpa," she said, going over and hugging him. "And I do understand. But I — I don't think Lou can." She swallowed, her eyes catching Ty's.

"You said you saw your father at the cemetery?" Scott asked her.

Amy nodded.

"Maybe Lou went there," he said abruptly. "She might have thought that he would go back." He took his car keys out of his pocket. "I'll go take a look."

"I'll come, too," Amy offered. At least then she would be doing something instead of just waiting around.

"OK," Scott said. He turned to Jack. "Call us if she comes back. I've got my phone. And we'll let you know if we find her."

❧

Scott's Jeep bumped down the driveway. Rain spattered onto the windshield, and the wipers beat methodically as they swung back and forth. Amy huddled deeper into her coat. *Please, please let us find Lou,* she prayed.

She glanced at Scott's face. The skin around his mouth and chin were taut with worry. "What was Jack thinking?" he muttered savagely, as they turned on to the road.

"He was just trying to do what he thought was best," Amy said hotly, jumping immediately to her grandpa's defense. "He didn't want us to get hurt."

"But he *knows* how Lou feels about your father," Scott said.

Amy didn't answer. She could see why Scott was siding with Lou, but she also saw her grandpa's side of things. It must have been awful for him to have watched Mom suffering after Daddy had left.

Daddy. The word seemed to ring in Amy's ears. She had seen her father — even spoken to him. An image of his face sprang into her mind. The deeply etched lines, the distant look in his eyes. She shut her eyes, willing it to go away.

Neither she nor Scott spoke again until they reached the cemetery. There were no lights on, and the wrought iron gates that led into the memorial ground were shut and locked. The mist from earlier had grown thicker, and now it swirled about the deserted parking lot. Suddenly, Amy caught sight of a single, lonely car parked under the leafless canopy of an oak tree.

"That's Lou's Honda!" she gasped.

Scott put his foot on the gas, and his Jeep shot across the parking lot, stopping with a screech of brakes behind Lou's car. Even before the Jeep had completely stopped, Amy was leaping out. She ran to the driver's door, her heart pounding.

The windows were frosted over, but Amy could just make out a shadowy figure, sitting huddled in the front seat.

"Lou!" she cried out, banging on the window.

The next moment, Amy saw her sister's face looking around at her.

Amy tried the door, but it was locked. "Open the door, Lou!"

For a moment, Lou didn't move, but then, with fumbling fingers, she released the catch.

Amy flung the door open. "We were so worried!"

Lou stared at her, her face white. "He wasn't here. I

waited and waited and he didn't come back." Suddenly, her face crumpled and a strangled sob burst from her. "Oh, Amy, I'm never going to see him again!"

Amy flung her arms around her sister's neck. "You will," she gabbled. "He'll get back in touch, and if he doesn't, we'll find him, Lou. I'll help you."

"You will?" Lou sobbed.

"Yes!" Amy felt prepared to say anything to comfort her sister. She was so relieved Lou was safe.

They hugged tightly.

"Lou! Are you all right?" Scott's deep voice spoke from behind Amy.

"Scott," Lou said, pulling back from Amy in confusion and looking up at him. "What are you doing here?"

"Jack told me what happened," Scott said quickly. "Are you OK?"

Lou nodded.

Scott crouched down and spoke softly. "You had us so worried." He took her hands. "You're freezing." He tightened his grip on her fingers. "Come on, let's get you home. We'll pick up your car tomorrow."

Lou looked too worn out to argue. She got out of the car without a word and allowed Scott to put his jacket over her shoulders. Wrapping an arm around her waist, he helped her into the Jeep.

The backseat was crowded with boxes of medicines, plastic gloves, and map books. Amy pushed them to one side and climbed in. The first wild rush of relief she had felt when they found Lou was fading, and she was beginning to feel anxious about what would happen when they got back home.

🙚

As soon as the Jeep drew up outside the house, the back door opened and Grandpa and Ty ran out. Amy had phoned them on Scott's cell phone to let them know that Lou was safe.

"Lou!" Grandpa exclaimed, hurrying over as Lou got out of the Jeep. "Thank heaven you're all right."

Lou ignored him and marched into the house without saying a word. With a look at her grandpa's hurt face, Amy ran after Lou.

"Lou!" she said, catching up with her sister in the kitchen. "Grandpa's been really worried about you."

Lou swung around, and Amy braced herself for a furious retort, but then Lou checked herself. When she spoke, her voice was quiet. "I'm not ready to talk to him right now, Amy," she said, the hurt showing in her eyes. "I just can't."

Scott, Grandpa, and Ty appeared in the doorway.

"I'm going to my room," Lou said bleakly.

"Lou," Grandpa said quickly, "we need to talk this through."

"There's nothing to discuss," Lou answered curtly.

She glanced at Scott. "Thanks for coming to find me," she said wearily. "I'll — I'll call you tomorrow."

Scott smiled. "Take care." He looked like he wanted to say more, but the presence of the others seemed to hold him back. "Get some rest," he said.

Lou nodded and then turned and walked out of the room.

There was a silence.

"I'd better go," Scott said at last. He glanced at Amy. "'Bye."

Amy felt tears rise in her eyes as he left. Everything was going wrong.

Ty put a hand on her shoulder. "Maybe it's best if I go, too," he said, looking at her and Jack. "You've got family things to sort out." He hugged Amy briefly. "I'll see you tomorrow."

Grandpa made an effort to smile. "Thanks for staying, Ty."

"No problem," Ty said. "I'm just glad nothing happened to Lou." With a last look at Amy, he left.

Grandpa sat down at the table. "Oh, Amy," he groaned, putting his head in his hands. "What am I going to do?"

Amy sat down beside him, wishing she could say something to comfort him. "It'll be OK," she managed. "Lou will come around in the end."

Grandpa looked up at her. "What about you? How do *you* feel? Do you want to meet your father?"

A vivid image of the man she had seen that afternoon at her mom's grave flashed into Amy's mind. She swallowed. "I didn't recognize him, Grandpa," she whispered. "I didn't know who he was."

"How could you?" Jack replied. "You haven't seen him for twelve years. You were only a toddler when he left."

Amy looked down. Maybe Grandpa was right, but it didn't make her feel any better. How could she not have known him? How could she not have felt even the faintest glimmer of recognition?

Jack took her hand. "Amy, you can't blame yourself for not knowing him. It's his fault for not being around when you were growing up."

Amy lifted worried eyes to his. "But —"

"There are no buts," Grandpa said firmly. He put his arms around her and hugged her tightly. "Your father chose to leave and to not stay in touch. It was his decision."

Amy felt the rough wool of his pullover rub against her cheek. "He did write to Mom that time," she said.

"Yes," Grandpa said quietly. "He did."

Amy glanced up at him. "Did — she ever tell you about that, Grandpa?" Until she and Lou had found the letter, she didn't have any idea that her father had ever written. How had Mom felt?

"She showed it to me the day it arrived," Grandpa said, the wrinkles on his face seeming to deepen as he remembered the time. "I — I was so angry with him."

He must have seen Amy's shocked look, because he shook his head. "So many years had passed. Your mom had built a new life for herself, she was just starting to find happiness, and then he wrote and almost destroyed everything again. Just the sight of his handwriting was enough to make her consider giving up everything she had here. She seriously thought about leaving and going back to him. She loved him, Amy. Despite everything he had done, she loved him to the end."

"But why didn't she go back?" Amy said wonderingly.

"I think she realized that whatever she and your father had once shared had been irreversibly spoiled. She knew that going back could never be the same," Grandpa replied. "After she showed me the letter, we didn't really discuss it any further. We both knew it was a decision she had to make on her own." He kissed the top of her head. "She made the right decision, Amy. For herself — and for the family."

Amy rested her head silently against him and thought about her mom. It must have been a painfully hard decision to make, especially if she had still loved him. And poor Grandpa. How awful it must have been for him, seeing what his daughter had gone through. Amy couldn't blame him for hating their father or for turning him away.

But Amy wasn't sure Lou would ever understand that.

Chapter Seven

The next morning, when Amy got up and went down-stairs to feed the horses, she found Grandpa already in the kitchen getting out the breakfast things. His eyes looked tired. "How did you sleep?" he asked.

Amy had slept restlessly, her dreams full of images of her father standing by her mother's grave. "Badly," she admitted, going over to the refrigerator.

"That makes two of us," Grandpa said.

Just then, the door opened and Lou came in. The air in the kitchen suddenly seemed to stiffen.

"Hi, Lou," Amy said, trying to act normal. "Do you want some orange juice?"

Lou shook her head. "No, thanks." She sat down at the table. She was dressed but looked tired and pale.

Grandpa put down the plates he had in his hand. "Did you sleep?" he asked her.

Lou shrugged. "On and off."

For a moment, Grandpa looked as if he was about to turn away, but then he changed his mind and sat down. "Look, Lou," he said. "I know what I did was wrong, but we can't let it come between us."

Amy watched her sister look at him with something resembling hope in her eyes.

"I've reached a decision," Grandpa continued. "Although I won't have your father here at Heartland, I can't — and I won't — stand in your way if you still want to find him."

Lou looked at him incredulously. "Did you really think you'd have been able to *stop* me?" she said, her voice rising.

"Lou —" Amy began, but her sister didn't even look at her. She had got to her feet and was staring at Grandpa.

"I'm not going to let you come between us again," she said angrily. "He's my father and I love him."

"I know you do, Lou," Jack Bartlett replied. "I'm just saying that I don't want him here at Heartland."

Lou shook her head and walked to the door. "I'm going to Scott's."

"You can't, Lou," Amy said, hurrying after her as she went outside. "Your car isn't here."

Lou paused for barely a second. "Then I'll walk," she said.

Grandpa joined Amy. "Don't be crazy, Lou. It's miles!"

For a fraction of a second, Amy thought that Lou was going to snap back, but she didn't; she just took a deep breath. "A walk will do me good," she said, her voice level. "I need some space."

Grandpa sighed. "Look, if you really want to go, Lou, I'll give you a lift. You can't walk all that way."

Lou hesitated, but just then both Ty's and Ben's cars came up the drive. A look of relief crossed her face. "It's OK," she said. "Ty will take me."

Lou hurried over to Ty's pickup and opened the passenger door, then the truck turned around and headed down the drive.

Grandpa turned and went into the house as Ben shut his car door and walked over. "What's going on?" he asked.

"Nothing," Amy snapped unhappily. She saw a hurt look cross Ben's face. Turning quickly, he marched up to the feed room. Amy kicked a nearby stone in frustration. Right now, she just didn't feel like coping with one of Ben's moods. Frowning, she followed him.

Ben was banging the buckets down onto the stone floor. Amy began to scoop grain into them. Neither of them spoke a word.

Eventually, Amy could stand the silence no longer. "I'll take these to the back barn," she said abruptly, picking up a pile of feed buckets. "You finish off here."

Ben didn't reply. Relieved to escape, Amy carried the feed buckets up the yard.

The horses in the barn were all looking over their doors. Seeing Amy, they whinnied excitedly.

"OK, OK, I'm here," Amy called, starting to empty the grain into the mangers. She reached Melody's stall last. The chestnut mare nickered softly as Amy came to her door.

"Hi, girl," Amy said, letting herself into the stall.

Melody nuzzled her shoulder as Amy tipped her feed into the manger. Amy let out a long sigh and watched the mare thrust her nose eagerly into the grain and begin to eat.

She put her arm around Melody's neck, taking comfort from the mare's warm, solid presence. Everything was so confusing. Grandpa and Lou had never argued like this before. She turned her face into the mare's rough mane.

She stood there for a moment and then felt warm breath on the back of her neck and looked around. As if sensing her unhappiness, Melody had turned her head to look at her. Lifting her nose, she gently nuzzled Amy's hair.

Amy swallowed. It was something her mom's horse, Pegasus, used to do before he'd died. Tears filled her eyes. "Oh, Melody," she whispered in despair. "I don't know which way to turn."

❧

T y arrived back just after Amy and Ben had finished feeding and watering the horses. "So what's going on?" he said curiously to Amy. "Lou hardly said a word on the way to Scott's."

"She had an argument with Grandpa this morning," Amy replied, trying to sound composed. "And last night."

"About your dad?" Ty asked.

Amy nodded her head.

"How are you doing?" Ty asked, looking at her in concern.

Before Amy could answer, the phone rang. "I'll get it," she said, knowing that Grandpa would probably be getting dressed.

She ran down the yard and into the kitchen. "Heartland," she said. "Amy Fleming here."

"Hi, this is Judy Stillman. I was wondering if I could speak to Ben."

"Just a second, I'll get him," Amy said. Seeing a wheelbarrow by Red's stall, she went over. "Your mom's on the phone," she called.

"I don't want to talk to her," Ben replied tersely. "Tell her I'm busy."

"Go and tell her yourself," Amy retorted angrily.

Ben glared at her. "I said I don't want to talk to her!"

It was the last straw. Amy's temper finally snapped.

"Oh, come on, Ben!" she yelled in exasperation. "Stop being so stubborn. Just go and talk to her."

"No!" Ben said furiously.

"Well, I'm not going to!" Amy yelled. "You can't put me in the middle of it."

Ty came hurrying over. "What's going on?" he demanded.

"He won't talk to his mom," Amy said, turning to Ty for support. "She's on the phone."

"Ben, you can't make Amy deal with your mom," Ty said curtly. "You have to do it yourself."

For a moment it looked as if Ben was about to argue, but then he turned and stormed down the yard to the house.

Amy watched him, but Ty just shook his head and went back to the chores.

Amy waited at the top of the stable block for Ben to finish with the call. She felt like she had to apologize to him for overreacting. But when Ben came back, he just grabbed his pitchfork and headed toward Red's stall, obviously ignoring Amy.

"Ben!" Amy exclaimed, going after him.

He swung around furiously. "Look, I spoke to her, didn't I? Now just leave me alone. I've got to get back to the stalls."

Amy was exhausted by her conflicting emotions. "Ben, just take a break for a second. I want to talk. Mucking out isn't really important right now."

Ben stiffened. "Oh, sorry, I forgot," he spat. "Nothing I do here is important, is it?"

"What are you talking about?" Amy demanded. She had no clue what he was getting at.

"Nothing I do matters!" Ben shouted. "You and Ty treat the horses, I'm just a stable hand. It doesn't matter how hard I work — I'm still an outsider. Basically, there's all of you — and then there's me."

Amy was completely taken aback. "But that's crazy," she said in astonishment. "We don't think that way."

"No?" Ben said disbelievingly. "So how come you never tell me what's going on?" Turning on his heel, he marched back to Red's stall.

Amy was stunned. She'd had no idea Ben was feeling so left out. She paused for a moment and then went after him.

He was angrily forking damp straw into the wheelbarrow.

"Ben," Amy said, but he didn't look up or even acknowledge her presence. "Look, I'm sorry," she said quickly. "I wasn't leaving you out on purpose. I just wasn't ready to talk about what's going on. It's kind of complicated."

Ben seemed to hesitate for a moment, but he still didn't look up.

Amy swallowed. "It's my dad," she said to his back. "You know how he left us twelve years ago? Well, Lou's been in touch with him recently, and he tried to visit the other day. He was the man Grandpa said was looking for work."

Ben turned quickly. "That guy?"

Amy nodded and quickly explained everything else that had happened. "So now Lou's mad, and Grandpa's determined not to let him come here," she concluded. She looked at his astonished face. "I — I told you it was complicated."

Ben nodded. "Yeah, I guess." The fire had faded completely from his eyes and he looked awkward. "Thanks for telling me."

"I should have told you before," Amy said. "You're part of Heartland now."

Ben looked away. "Yeah, whatever," he muttered, not sounding as if he believed her.

"You *are*," Amy insisted.

Ben shrugged and turned back to the straw bed. After watching him for a few moments longer, Amy shook her head and walked away.

She found Ty in the back barn. "Still in one piece?" he said with a grin.

Amy was in no mood to be teased. She told him quickly about what Ben had said. "He doesn't feel like he's important here," she said.

"That doesn't make sense," Ty said.

"It's what he thinks," Amy replied. "I explained to him

what's going on with Lou and Grandpa, but it didn't seem to make much of a difference."

Ty frowned. "We should talk to him."

"I tried," Amy said, "but he's not in the mood to listen."

"We can try again later," Ty said. "You could say you need someone to ride Gypsy and go on the trails with him. It might be easier to get him to talk away from here."

Amy nodded. "OK, but what about you? Will you come?"

Ty shook his head. "I think it's better if I don't. He'll open up more if it's just the two of you."

✥

Two hours later, Amy and Ben rode away from Heartland on Moochie and Gypsy. The wind had picked up, and the horses jogged excitedly. Amy patted Moochie's bay neck. "Let's go on the field trail," she said. "It'll be more sheltered than up on the mountain."

Ben nodded, and they turned onto the trail that led down into the valley. They rode along the grassy path in silence. Amy tried to think of a way to begin the conversation she wanted to have, but whenever she glanced at Ben, the sight of his set profile made the words die on her tongue. What could she say? However she started, it was going to be a very awkward discussion.

Moochie pulled at his reins, and Amy decided to put off the conversation. "Want to trot?" she asked.

"OK," Ben said shortly.

Amy clicked her tongue, and Moochie leaped eagerly into a trot. The trees on either side of the trail were swaying in the wind, and Moochie's mane blew over Amy's hands. She looked across at Gypsy. The black mare was throwing up her head, looking as if she wanted to go faster, but Ben controlled her effortlessly.

"Gypsy's going well for you," Amy called.

They trotted around a bend in the path. Suddenly both Moochie and Gypsy shied violently. A pile of barrels covered with a plastic tarp had been left standing at the side of the trail. The tarp flapped wildly in the wind, making a thunderous noise.

Quickly recovering her balance, Amy brought Moochie under control and glanced over at Ben. He was soothing Gypsy, who was backing away from the barrels, trembling.

"It's OK, girl," Amy heard him saying. "They won't hurt you."

"I'll pass them first," Amy called, hoping that if Gypsy saw Moochie walk past the barrels, she would follow. She closed her legs on Moochie's sides. "Walk on," she said. But just as the big bay stepped forward, the tarp flapped furiously, and Moochie shied back again.

"Here, I'll try it," Ben said. Shortening his reins, he

urged Gypsy on. The black mare snorted, her eyes wide. But Ben insisted. Lifting her feet high, Gypsy approached the barrels, every muscle in her body tense.

Just then, a huge gust of wind blew under the tarp and tore it free from the weight of the barrel. It twirled upward. With a frightened whinny, Gypsy plunged sideways, but the wind whipped the tarp toward her, and the next moment it was caught between her back legs.

With a terrified snort, Gypsy began to buck viciously.

"Ben!" Amy gasped in horror.

Gypsy's bucking had allowed the tarp to escape from her legs, and it was now twirling away across the field. But Gypsy seemed oblivious. With her head between her knees, she was still bucking wildly.

Amy's stomach somersaulted. There was no way Ben could stay on. She waited for him to come crashing to the ground. But he didn't. His body moved with the horse, his strong legs and seat anchoring him in the saddle. After three more bucks, he managed to pull Gypsy's head up. Amy saw his lips moving constantly as he sought to quiet the frightened mare. At long last, she came to a trembling halt.

"Are you OK, Ben?" Amy exclaimed, nudging Moochie and trotting forward.

Ben was leaning low over Gypsy's neck, his hands stroking and soothing as he calmed her down. He looked around.

"That was exciting," he said with a grin.

Amy stared at him in amazement. After what he had just been through, how could he smile like that? "How did you stay on?" she stammered.

"Guess it's just this special glue that I use," Ben joked.

"If you'd fallen off we'd have been back to square one," Amy said, suddenly realizing how lucky they'd been that Ben had stayed on and that all their work with Gypsy hadn't been ruined. "That was amazing!"

Ben suddenly looked embarrassed. "It's no big deal," he said awkwardly.

"Yes, it is!" Amy exclaimed.

But Ben didn't look convinced. "Anyone could have stayed on."

"That's not true," Amy said. "Ben! You're a great rider." She saw the doubt on his face, and all the words that she had been wanting to say tumbled out of her. "You don't realize how much work you saved us by staying on. I don't know why you feel like you're not a real part of Heartland. You really are, and if it took a wild mare almost throwing you off for me to convince you, then I guess it's a good thing."

Ben hesitated for a moment, trying to take in everything Amy had said. "Do you mean that?"

"Yes!" Amy cried. "We really need you. And we want you to feel like part of the team."

A flush of color crossed Ben's face. "Thanks," he said. "That really means a lot, Amy."

"It's the truth," she said simply. She grinned at him. "You're one of us now — whether you like it or not."

To her relief, Ben smiled back. "Sounds good to me," he said.

They exchanged smiles, and then Ben picked up his reins and asked Gypsy to walk on. "Looks like you were right about her," he said, changing the subject quickly. "She's not ready to go home yet."

"Definitely not," Amy agreed as she rode along the trail beside him. "So, are you looking forward to the show?" she asked, happy to go along with the change of subject now that the tension between them had subsided.

Ben nodded. "Yeah, I am. You and Soraya are still going to come, aren't you?"

"Of course," Amy said.

They rode on for a few more minutes in silence and then Ben spoke. "You — you know when my mom called this morning?" he said.

Amy nodded. How could she forget!

"Well, she said she can make it to the show after all," Ben said. "She's changed her meeting."

"That's great!" Amy exclaimed. She saw the frown on his face. "Isn't it?" she asked uncertainly.

Ben looked down at Gypsy's neck. "It's to the point that I don't care what she does," he said. "She doesn't care about me."

Amy stared at him. "But she's your mom."

"So?" Ben said. He shook his head bitterly. "I've never meant anything to her."

"I can't believe that's true," Amy said, thinking about the hurt in Mrs. Stillman's voice the day Ben had refused to speak to her on the phone.

Ben said, "Then why did she send me to live with my aunt? She just wanted me out of the way."

"I thought it was because you were getting into trouble," Amy said, remembering what she had been told about Ben's past. "You know, skipping school and stuff." She stared at his face. "If she didn't care, she wouldn't have done anything, Ben. It can't have been easy for her."

"Well, it wasn't easy for me, either!" Ben exclaimed with a sudden burst of anger. He shook his head. "It's not like I could make you understand. You can't know how hard it is. Your mom never abandoned you!" Almost before the words were out he seemed to regret them. He paled, but Amy hardly noticed. She was too angry.

"No! But my dad did!" she retorted with bitterness. "*My* mom's dead." Hot tears sprang to her eyes. "You don't know how lucky you are, Ben!" she yelled. "I can't believe you won't give her another chance."

Desperate to hide her tears, Amy dug her heels into Moochie's side. With a surprised snort, he leaped forward into a canter. Amy urged him on. She heard Ben yell at her to stop, but she ignored him. She wanted to get away from him — away from everything.

She pounded her legs against Moochie's sides, but no matter how fast he ran, images of her mother's and father's faces flashed before her eyes.

Moochie's canter became a gallop, his hooves pounding across the damp grass. The wind buffeted Amy's face, whipping tears from her eyes. She dug her heels in, trying to escape Ben, trying to escape everyone.

Through the mist of tears, Amy could see a sharp turn at the end of the path. She knew that they would never make it at such high speed, but for one wild moment she didn't care. Ben, Lou, Grandpa, Daddy — the only way to forget them was to keep going faster.

Suddenly, she heard the sound of hooves behind her. She glanced over her shoulder. Urged on by Ben, Gypsy was drawing near. Ben leaned low over the black mare's neck. "Amy, stop!" he yelled. "You can't make that turn!"

Ignoring him, Amy urged Moochie forward, the corner becoming impossibly close. In three powerful strides, Gypsy had caught up. Leaning over her neck, Ben grabbed at Moochie's reins.

Feeling the reins yank on his mouth, Moochie jerked his head up, his haunches skidding underneath him.

Amy was flung back in the saddle, and it was only by grasping a handful of Moochie's mane that she kept herself from falling off.

"What are you doing?" she screamed at Ben.

"Me?" he yelled back. "What about you?"

Amy was about to defend herself when suddenly she saw the corner, only a stride ahead of them, and realized how close she had come to hurting Moochie. At that speed, crashing off the path would have been devastating. Amy's emotions, stretched taut by the events of the last few days, snapped, and a sob burst from her. Scrambling down from Moochie's back, she collapsed on the ground and buried her head in her hands.

Within a few seconds, Ben had dismounted and was kneeling next to her. "It's OK," he said, putting an arm on her trembling shoulder. "Amy, I'm sorry. I just wasn't thinking. I've got a lot of things to work out. I'm sorry I brought you into it."

"It's not you," Amy said distraught. "It's everything — everything's gone wrong."

"Things will work out," Ben said. "You'll see."

"How can they?" Amy cried. "Grandpa and Lou are never going to agree about my dad. What if he comes back? What if Lou decides to leave Heartland and live with him?"

"That won't happen," Ben said. But Amy knew they were empty words. Who could tell what was going to happen in the future? And who knew what would happen if Daddy did come back? Her tears fell faster.

Powerless to say anything to comfort her, Ben kept his hand on her shoulder, gently rubbing until, at long last, her sobs started to subside. Amy took a deep breath and raised her head to look at him. "I'm sorry," she said, feeling horribly embarrassed. She rubbed her jacket sleeve across her face.

"Don't be," Ben said. "It's my fault. I'm too caught up in my problems. I forgot you've got your own things to deal with."

"It's OK," Amy said. She glanced at him and swallowed. There was something she had to say. "It's just hard sometimes. I can't help but think about how much I miss my mom whenever we talk about yours."

She saw Ben flinch and looked away. There was a long silence. Finally, Amy gathered up the reins and put her foot in the stirrup. "Come on," she said, not looking at him. "We should go."

She mounted. When she looked around, she saw that Ben was still standing beside Gypsy.

"Ben?" she said. "You ready?"

He didn't answer her question right away. "Yeah," he said quietly. "I guess I'm ready."

Not saying anything more, he mounted and clicked his tongue. The two horses moved forward.

They rode in silence. Ben seemed to be thinking about

something, but Amy hardly noticed. Her own thoughts had moved to the issue of Lou and Grandpa and the situation at home.

As they approached the barns, the two horses broke off, each heading to its stall. As they parted, Ben turned in his saddle. There was a decisive look on his face. "I'm going to go call my mom," he said.

Amy pulled herself out of her own thoughts and stared at him. "You are?"

"Yeah." Ben took a deep breath. "I was thinking that it doesn't matter what's happened, she's still my mom. And if she wants to come to the show, then it would be nice if she could be there."

Chapter Eight

Amy was untacking Moochie when Ty came to find her. "How did it go?" he asked her in a low voice.

After everything that had happened, Amy had almost forgotten that the reason for the ride had been to reassure Ben about the importance of his role at Heartland. "OK," she said. "I — I think we sorted things out."

"Good," Ty said, looking relieved.

"I'll tell you about it later," Amy said, letting herself out of the stall.

As Amy headed to the tack room, she heard Ben talking in Red's stall. She glanced in as she walked by and saw him on his cell phone. *All right,* Amy thought to herself, hoping the conversation with his mom was going well.

"So?" she demanded, stopping at the stall door when she heard him say good-bye. "How did it go?"

He shrugged. "Well, I told her she could come to the show."

"And she's going to?" Amy asked eagerly, shifting the weight of Moochie's saddle in her arms.

Ben nodded. "She's meeting me there." He ran a hand through his hair. "That's going to be fun," he said with sarcasm.

"It'll be fine," Amy said optimistically.

But Ben looked far from convinced.

Well, it may not have been a full-blown reconciliation, she thought as she walked away from Red's stall, *but at least Ben is speaking to his mom again — surely that's a step in the right direction.*

❧

For the rest of the day, Ben was like a different person around the yard. He laughed and joked and even came down to the house to have lunch with Amy and Ty.

"Well, whatever you said to him must have worked," Ty said to Amy that afternoon as they both filled water buckets at the faucet. "He's never been so relaxed."

Amy then told Ty about how Gypsy had shied when the tarp ripped free and about her conversation with Ben afterward, but she didn't say anything about the way she had taken off on Moochie. She felt ashamed of her reaction and wanted to forget what she had done.

"Best of all, he got in touch with his mom," Amy said. "She's going to meet us at the show next week."

"So you're still planning to go and watch?" Ty asked.

"Yes," Amy said. "Why don't you come?"

"I'd like to," Ty replied. "But I'm meeting some friends — it's my day off."

Amy looked at him in shock. Ty hardly ever went out unless it was to do something with horses. "Who are you meeting?" she asked.

"Pete and Greg. They're friends of mine from high school," Ty said. "We've been planning it for a while — a kind of reunion before they go off to college. I would have liked to have made it to the show, though. I hope Ben does well. He's been working so hard with Red — he really deserves it. I can't believe how much they've improved."

Just then, the farmhouse door opened and Grandpa looked out. "Amy!" he called. "Phone call! It's Mr. Phillips!"

Amy ran down to the kitchen and took the phone from her grandpa. "Hi," she said. "Amy speaking."

She heard the hesitancy in Mr. Phillips's voice. "I — I was just calling to find out how Melody is," he said. "I hope you don't mind."

"Not at all," Amy said. She hadn't spoken to him since just after Melody's accident. She had meant to call him, but the events of the last few days has pushed all other thoughts out of her mind. Now she was glad to be able to give him good news. "She's doing really well," she said. "Her wound's healing, and she's not showing any sign of going into labor." She remembered the best news of all. "And we've felt her foal kick, which means it's alive."

"Oh, how wonderful," Ray Phillips gasped. Amy heard him take a deep, trembling breath. "I've been so worried," he admitted.

"Well, like I said, she's doing fine," Amy said.

"My wife would have been pleased," Mr. Phillips said quietly.

Amy heard the note of sadness in his voice. "Will you come and see the foal when it's born?" she asked.

"I'd love to," Ray Phillips replied. He paused. When he spoke again it was with difficulty. "Maybe if I could just see for myself that Melody and her foal are OK, then I'd feel that I did the right thing after all."

"I'll call you and let you know as soon as the foal is born," Amy promised. "And, Mr. Phillips," she added quickly, "I'm sure everything will be just fine."

When she put the phone down, she was thinking hard. Mr. Phillips obviously still blamed himself for Melody's accident. She hoped that Melody's foal would be healthy, so Mr. Phillips could see for himself that everything had worked out. She hoped with all her heart that Melody and her foal were going to make it.

❧

Lou came back from Scott's that evening, but she hardly spoke to Grandpa. As the next few days passed, the silences between them grew longer. There were no more arguments, but the tension in the air was apparent. Lou was determined to find their father. She called all the hotels and lodges in the area to see if he'd been staying there, but apart from the time she was on the phone she avoided being in the house, spending her time in the yard with Ben and Ty, or going out with Scott.

For the first time in her life, Amy found herself almost looking forward to going to school each day; at least it meant she could escape from the atmosphere at Heartland. She longed to be able to do something about the growing rift between Grandpa and Lou but didn't know what she could do. Grandpa was adamant about not having their father at Heartland, and Lou was equally determined to track him down.

On Friday afternoon, Lou was waiting expectantly when Amy got home from school. "I think I've found where Daddy was staying," she said, her eyes sparkling. "There was a Tim Fleming staying at a place called the River House Inn. He checked out on Sunday."

Amy stared at her. With each day that had passed, she

had begun to think, with relief, that Lou wasn't going to be able to track their father down. "Was it definitely Daddy?" she stammered.

"I don't know," Lou said excitedly. "But I'm sure it must be. The name's right, and they said he was tall with dark hair and that he checked in there the day before Daddy visited here. They didn't know where he was going to next, but they have an address for him."

"Are — are you going to write to him again?" Amy asked.

"I already have," Lou replied. "I sent a letter off this afternoon. I told him that we were both desperate to see him." She must have seen the shock on Amy's face because she frowned. "Why are you looking like that? You told me that you wanted to find him. You told me that you'd *help* me."

Amy remembered her words the night that she and Scott had found Lou outside the cemetery. "I know," she said, trying to appease Lou. "And I do want you to find him, it's just —"

She broke off as Grandpa came into the room. The effect on Lou was immediate; a shutter seemed to fall across her face. "Well, I'll let you know if there's any news," she said abruptly to Amy, and then she turned and left the kitchen.

Amy looked at her grandpa. She didn't know what to say. The longer the argument went on, the less likely it looked that it would ever be resolved. She couldn't understand why they hadn't made up.

"Did — did Lou tell you she thinks she's found where Daddy was staying?" she asked.

"No," Jack said, looking shocked.

"She's got an address for him, and she's already written to him again," Amy said.

Jack shook his head. There was a moment's silence between them.

"Grandpa," Amy whispered suddenly, "I don't want to see him."

Jack looked at her and then held out his arms. "Come here," he said.

Amy stepped forward and felt his arms close around her, warm and comforting.

"You know, you have to make that decision for yourself, but whatever you decide," he said softly, "I'll always be here for you, no matter what."

✖

Five minutes later, Amy was headed up the yard — she'd decided getting back to her chores was the best way to distract herself from what Lou had told her. It was cold outside, and she was glad of her warm jacket.

Seeing Ty come out of the tack room, she jogged up to meet him. "Have you checked on Melody today?" she asked.

"She's a bit restless," Ty replied, "but I've walked her around several times and that seems to have calmed her down a bit."

Amy nodded. Scott had told them that it was likely that Melody would get livelier as her wound healed and the infection went down. He'd also said that, all being well, they could start letting her out to graze for a few hours each day the following week.

"I'll go and see her," Amy said.

Just then, Ben appeared, leading Red down from the training ring.

"How was he?" Ty called.

"Great," Ben replied, stopping and patting Red's powerful neck. "We just worked on the flat so he can save his energy for tomorrow."

"I bet he'll be totally fabulous," Amy said confidently. "Are you going to bathe him?"

Ben glanced at the gray sky and shook his head. "I think it's too cold. I'll just wash his tail and give the rest of him a really good brushing. I'll braid him in the morning." He clicked his tongue and went on down the yard.

"The forecast says there could be snow in the next few days," Ty commented as he and Amy continued to Melody's stall.

"I hope it holds off until after the show," Amy said, shivering.

Ty nodded.

They reached the back barn. Melody was looking out over her door. "Have you been restless today?" Amy said, stroking the mare's warm neck and looking at her churned-up bed. "I could take her for another walk," she decided out loud.

"Sure," Ty replied. "I'll fix her bedding while she's out of the stall."

Amy slipped Melody's halter on and led the mare down the drive. Melody's pregnant belly seemed bigger than ever. It was hard to believe that she still had another two weeks to go before the foal was due. She walked slowly and heavily, and Amy noticed that her legs had filled up with fluid again.

"Poor girl," she said to the mare. "You'll be happier when you can go out and graze for a bit each day, won't you? That exercise will keep the swelling down."

She paused to let Melody nibble at the grass, but to her surprise, the mare didn't seem hungry. She tore at a few strands and then lost interest.

Amy decided to take her back to her stall. She bumped into Ben, who was carrying Red's tack. He frowned. "She looks close to foaling," he said.

Amy stopped Melody. "You think so?" she questioned anxiously. "She's still got two weeks to go."

"I'd say no more than a week, maximum," Ben said.

"Look at her hindquarters — all her muscles have slackened off. That normally only happens a few days before labor starts."

Feeling worried, Amy led Melody up to the barn and into her stall. What if Ben was right and Melody had her foal early? She would call Scott and give him a heads-up.

"He may be right," Scott replied when she got through to him and told him what Ben had said. "But don't worry. It's not really too early for her to have her foal. Mares rarely give birth on the day they're supposed to. Going into labor a couple of weeks either side of their due date is considered normal. The foal's health won't be at risk if it is born now."

"Will you come see her?" Amy asked, feeling slightly reassured. "Just to make sure?"

"I've got a really busy couple of days, I'm afraid," Scott said. "Why don't you see how it goes and give me a call if you get worried. Otherwise I'll try to come on Sunday."

❧

There was a thick frost on the ground when Amy got up early the next morning. As she strode up the yard, she glanced at the gray sky. The clouds looked like they were heavy with snow. She frowned, hoping that it would hold off at least until after the show.

Melody was walking restlessly around her stall. Amy went in and ran her hands over the mare's sides and hindquarters. Her muscles felt soft.

"How is she?"

Amy turned and saw Ben standing by the door. "You're here early," she said in surprise.

"I didn't sleep that well," he replied. "I couldn't stop thinking about the show — and about seeing my mom."

"Well, Melody seems about the same as yesterday," Amy said, patting the chestnut mare. "She still seems restless." She frowned. "Maybe I shouldn't go to the show, after all. Maybe I should stay here."

"But you've got to come," Ben said quickly. "I need your support. The showground's only an hour away," he added. "Can't you ask your grandpa to keep an eye on Melody? If anything happens he can call us on my cell phone and we'll come right back."

Amy felt torn, but she reluctantly agreed. "OK, if Grandpa doesn't mind."

Jack was preparing breakfast in the kitchen. He frowned as she came in. "You look worried, honey," he said. "Is everything OK?"

Amy explained about Melody. "I'm really not sure about leaving her, but Ben really wants me to go to the show."

"You go," Grandpa said immediately. "I can keep an eye on Melody. If there's any change, I'll call you right away." He seemed to see the uncertainty on Amy's face. "Don't worry about it. I might not have experienced many mares foaling, but I've seen plenty of calvings. If worst comes to worst, I'll be able to hold the fort until Scott gets here."

Amy still felt torn, but deep down she knew he was right. Grandpa had years of experience with farm animals. If anything happened, he would know what to do. "Thanks, Grandpa," she said. "I'll tell Ben I can go."

Soraya arrived at eight-thirty. "Hey!" Amy called, coming out of Jake's stall.

"Hi," Soraya replied. She waved good-bye to her mom and ran up the yard to meet Amy. "So what can I do?" she asked, dumping her bag on the ground.

"Take your pick," Amy said. "There are the stalls in the other barn to finish and all the horses to water, and someone needs to walk Melody. We're going to have to work pretty hard, because Ben is busy getting Red groomed and braided. We're leaving for the show at noon."

Soraya immediately went to find a pitchfork and started helping Amy with Jake's stall. "Where's Ben now?" she asked.

"In the barn," Amy replied. She thought about the

way he had been hurrying through his chores that morning. "I think he's a bit nervous."

Just then, Ben came to Jake's stall. "The stalls in the barn are done," he said to Amy. "Is it OK if I braid Red now?"

"Sure," Amy said. "Soraya and I will finish off the stalls down here."

"Great," Ben said, and jogged off.

"He does look nervous," Soraya commented to Amy in a low voice.

Amy nodded as she watched Ben disappear into the tack room. She desperately hoped everything was going to go well for him that day — both in the ring *and* with his mom.

Chapter Nine

At noon, Amy, Soraya, and Ben loaded Red into the trailer and got into the pickup. Grandpa came out of the house to wave them off.

"Good luck!" he called out as Ben started the engine.

Amy took one last glance toward the back barn and Melody's stall. She hated leaving her but knew she could trust Grandpa.

They reached the showground an hour before the class was due to start. Ben carefully steered the trailer through the horses and ponies milling around and found a quiet corner to park. "I'll go and sign in," he said, jumping out of the pickup.

"Do you want us to get Red out for you?" Amy asked.

Ben nodded. "Yeah, thanks."

Soraya lowered the ramp while Amy went into the

trailer. As the ramp went down, Red let out a piercing whinny. The muscles on his neck were tense with excitement, and he danced out of the trailer beside Amy, his head held high.

While Amy held him, Soraya removed the protective wraps from his legs. He sidestepped excitedly.

"I think we'd better walk him around to calm him down," Amy said, seeing the damp patches of sweat darkening his neck.

"Do you think Ashley will be here?" Soraya asked as they put on Red's bridle.

"Probably," Amy said, making a face at the thought. Ashley Grant was in their class at school. Her parents owned a hunter barn — Greenbriar — and Ashley rode in shows nearly every weekend. The horses and ponies she rode were always expensive and very well trained. She and Amy had often competed against each other in the Large Pony Hunter classes, where, much to Ashley's disgust, Sundance had carried off the blue ribbon a good bit of the time.

However, as Amy and Soraya walked Red around the showground, they didn't see Ashley or her family.

They had just begun to tack Red up when Ben returned with his number.

"All right," he said, "the classes are running on time so I should start warming him up."

"He's kind of high-strung," Soraya commented.

"He always is when he comes to a show," Ben said, patting Red's gleaming neck. "He loves them." He glanced down at his jeans. "I need to get changed, too," he said. "Can you walk him around a little longer?"

Amy nodded. "At your command — we'll do whatever you need."

Soraya giggled as Ben disappeared into the living quarters of his trailer. "You said it!"

Amy chucked Red's bell boots at her. "Put these on!" she said with a grin. "And quit dreaming!"

Five minutes later, Ben came out of the trailer. Amy thought she was going to have to physically shut Soraya's mouth for her, it dropped open so far. Ben's jeans and barn jacket were gone, and in their place were spotless tan breeches, long leather boots, and a beautifully cut black show jacket. Even though Ben wasn't Amy's type, she had to admit that he looked very nice.

Seemingly oblivious to their reactions, Ben walked over to Red. "Thanks for tacking him up," he said, taking the reins.

"That's OK," Amy said, realizing that Soraya was incapable of speech.

Ben mounted. "I'll go and warm up," he said.

Amy and Soraya watched Ben ride off, Red prancing, his powerful muscles clearly defined under his glossy chestnut coat, Ben sitting effortlessly in the saddle. They looked perfect together.

"Wow! And I never thought I'd find a cute, nice guy who likes horses," Soraya breathed.

Amy gave her friend a knowing smile. "Come on, let's go and watch."

They found a space at the side of the schooling ring and watched Ben start to work Red. The ring was busy, with horses and ponies cantering around in all directions and several trainers standing in the middle, shouting out instructions. But Ben managed to find a reasonably quiet corner and began to get Red warmed up.

Suddenly, Soraya nudged Amy. "It's Ashley! Look!"

Amy glanced around. Ashley Grant was trotting into the ring on a beautiful bay hunter. Her long platinum-blond hair was tied back in a single braid, and her perfectly tailored navy show jacket accentuated her tall, slim figure. The only thing that marred the picture was the scowl on Ashley's face.

"Out of my way!" she snapped at a younger girl who was getting ready to jump one of the practice fences. Barging the bay hunter past the girl's gray pony, Ashley cantered toward the jump. The bay sailed over it, his dark coat gleaming. Ashley smiled smugly as if she was aware of exactly how good she looked.

"How come she always has such lovely horses?" Soraya said. "It's totally unfair."

Amy nodded. She wouldn't have swapped Sundance for anything, but Ashley did get to ride the most amazing horses. For a moment, Amy wished she had Sundance there so that she could at least attempt to wipe the self-satisfied smile off Ashley's face.

Just then, Ashley turned and saw them. "Oh, no!" Amy groaned under her breath as Ashley turned her horse and began to trot toward them. "How could she have spotted us?"

"It must be an evil sixth sense," Soraya whispered.

Ashley stopped along the fence rail. "What are you two doing here?" she said, as if they had no right to be at a show.

"What do you think?" Amy retorted.

"Well, you're obviously not competing," Ashley said, sweeping her green eyes disparagingly over their yard clothes. "Not even *you* would go in a ring looking like that, Amy."

Before Amy could reply, Ben came trotting over. "Can you take Red for me?" he said to Amy and Soraya. "I want to go and have a look at the course." Suddenly he seemed to notice Ashley. "Oh, sorry," he said quickly. "I didn't mean to interrupt."

"You haven't interrupted *anything*," Amy said pointedly.

"Of course we'll hold Red," Soraya said, jumping over the fence.

Ashley was looking at Ben. "Hi," she said, her lips curving into a smile. "I don't think we've met before. I'm Ashley Grant, and you're —"

"Ben Stillman," Ben said dismounting. "I work at Heartland." He held out his hand. "Nice to meet you, Ashley."

"And you," Ashley replied.

"Well, I'd better go walk the course," Ben said. "See you around."

"You can count on it," Ashley purred, giving him a little wave as he walked off.

Amy glanced at Soraya. She was biting her lip as she checked Red's girth.

"Ashley!" a voice bellowed. Ashley swung around. Her mother, Val Grant, was making her way through the crowd, a frown on her square-jawed face. "What are you doing?" she shouted. "Why aren't you working Dreamtime in?"

Ashley turned abruptly to Amy and Soraya. "See you, then," she said coldly, and cantered off.

"Can you believe Ashley?" Soraya exclaimed the second she was out of earshot. "Did you hear how she was cooing at Ben?"

Amy nodded. "He didn't seem that interested, though," she said quickly.

"I guess." Soraya sighed. "I just wish he was interested in *me*."

❧

After ten minutes, Ben came back from walking the course.

"What's it like?" Amy asked.

"Not too bad," Ben replied. He glanced at his watch.

"What time did your mom say she'd be here?" Amy asked, guessing what was on his mind.

"Three-thirty," Ben said shortly. "Fifteen minutes ago."

"I'm sure she'll make it," Soraya said reassuringly. "She probably just ran into traffic."

"Or she decided not to come," Ben said tersely. He swung himself back into the saddle. "I'd better keep Red moving. We're jumping fifth in the order." Without another word, he rode off.

Amy watched him trot around the schooling area, his eyes scanning the crowds. *Please let his mom get here on time*, she thought desperately.

The loudspeaker crackled and announced that the High Preliminary class was about to begin.

"Do we have a cloth to dust off Red before he goes in?" Soraya asked suddenly.

Amy shook her head.

"I'll run back to the trailer and get one," Soraya said. She ran off through the throngs of people and horses.

Amy looked around, hoping Ben's mom would appear. In the training ring, Ben turned Red toward a practice fence, but he didn't seem to be concentrating, and Red's forelegs clattered into the top rail. Glad for something to do, Amy slid between the fence boards, walked quickly into the ring, and put the fence up again.

"Thanks," Ben said, his face grim.

Dodging the cantering horses and shouting trainers, Amy went back to the fence. She saw Ben trying to canter Red in a figure eight, but the horse appeared to sense his owner's tension and threw his head up, fighting for the reins.

"And coming into the ring we have number 381," the loudspeaker announced.

"Ben!" Amy called. "You're in the hole."

Ben rode Red toward her. Despite the cold, the chestnut was sweating. He tossed his head in agitation.

Just then Soraya appeared. "Here, I have a cloth. I'll rub him down," she offered.

Ben's face relaxed for a second. "Thanks, Soraya," he said as she started to rub the sweat marks away from Red's side.

"That's OK," Soraya said, smiling up at him.

Ben looked at them both. "Thanks for coming today, you guys. It's good to have the support."

Amy heard a hard edge to his voice and realized he was thinking about his mom.

The loudspeaker crackled into life. "That was four faults for number 381, and now we have number 382 in the ring."

"You'd better get to the ring," Amy said quickly. "You're two away."

Ben nodded and took up his reins.

As Red stepped forward, a voice called out. "Ben!"

Ben swung around abruptly. "Mom!" he exclaimed.

A woman was hurrying through the crowd toward them. The thick blond hair that fell around her shoulders was exactly the same shade as Ben's, and her blue eyes were the mirror image of his.

"I got held up on the way here," she gasped. "I thought I wasn't going to make it."

"Well, it wouldn't be the first time," Ben said, his voice suddenly cool. "Something came up at work?"

"No," Judy Stillman said, looking at him in surprise. "I told you, I canceled my meeting today. It was the snow. It's really falling north of here."

"It's snowing!" Soraya said.

As Judy Stillman nodded, the loudspeaker made an announcement. "Will number 384 come to the collecting ring, please. Number 384."

"Ben! That's you!" Amy exclaimed.

Ben seemed to hesitate for a moment.

"Go on," his mom said. "We can talk later. I want to see you jump."

Amy saw some of the tension leave Ben's face.

"Number 384!" the loudspeaker said.

Ben loosened his reins and Red plunged forward.

"Good luck!" Soraya called excitedly.

Ben turned in his saddle. "Thanks!" he shouted, and then he jogged Red toward the collecting ring.

"I'm Amy Fleming," Amy said to Mrs. Stillman, realizing that they hadn't been introduced. "And this is my friend Soraya Martin."

"Judy Stillman," Ben's mom said. "It's nice to meet you both. I really thought I wasn't going to get here."

"We'd better go into the arena," Soraya said quickly, "or we'll miss Ben's round."

They hurried to the viewing gallery of the indoor arena, found three empty seats, and sat down.

"Our first clear round," the announcer said as the rider before Ben rode out of the arena to a round of applause. "And now we have number 384, Ben Stillman, riding What Luck."

"Here he is!" Amy exclaimed, grabbing Soraya's arm.

Ben came trotting into the arena on Red. He looked calm and utterly focused, his lips moving inaudibly as he spoke quietly to the horse. Red seemed to mirror his rider's confidence. Amy crossed her fingers. They just *had* to do well.

The starting bell rang out, and Ben turned Red toward the first fence, a solid green-and-white oxer. Amy leaned forward in her seat as the chestnut approached it smoothly. She was so nervous it felt as if she were riding the course herself, as if she could feel every stride Red was taking. Ben met the jump perfectly and Red soared over it, his forelegs snapping up neatly.

Then he was cantering toward the gate. He sailed over that and then over the upright, the wall, the red-and-blue double, another oxer, and finally turned toward the treble. As he approached the line of three jumps, Amy held her breath. "Go on!" She breathed, knowing that if he could just clear this last combination, he would be in the jump-off. "Go on!"

Red took off over the first. He cleared it. He seemed to hesitate, but Ben sat down in the saddle and drove him on, and in one stride he was over the second. Again he seemed to falter as he approached the third, but Ben urged him on and Red responded. Taking two neat strides, he cleared the final fence.

"Yes!" Amy and Soraya exclaimed in delight as the audience broke into a round of applause.

"And that's a clear round for Ben Stillman on What Luck," the announcer said over the clapping.

Amy was totally delighted. "He's in the jump-off!" she cried, turning to Ben's mom.

Judy Stillman's eyes were shining with pride. "He was wonderful!"

Soraya jumped to her feet. "Let's go and find him!"

Quickly, they made their way outside. Ben had

jumped off Red and was patting the chestnut as if he were never going to stop.

Amy raced up to him. "Nice round!" she gasped, patting Red, too.

"Wasn't he amazing?" Ben said to her, his eyes filled with happiness. "He didn't touch a single rail."

Soraya reached them. "Way to go, Ben!" she cried.

Caught up in the moment, Ben gave her a hug. "We're in the jump-off, Soraya!" he exclaimed.

Amy saw the look of shock on her friend's face as Ben hugged her. However, it was quickly replaced by a smile of utter elation. "You were amazing!" Soraya said.

"Oh, Ben."

Hearing his mom's voice, Ben pulled away from Soraya and turned. Judy Stillman was standing behind him, her eyes shining with delighted tears. "You looked great. I'm so proud of you," she said.

"Really?" Ben said, frowning suddenly.

Judy Stillman looked at him in surprise. "Of course! You rode a wonderful round." She looked at him for a moment and then shook her head. "Why wouldn't I be proud?"

"I've just never heard you say anything like that before," Ben said.

"That's not true, Ben," Judy protested.

"Are you sure?" Ben said, his voice suddenly cold. "I can't remember the last time you watched me ride."

"Ben," Judy began, "I know the last eight years have been hard for you, but you have to believe me, I've only ever done what I thought was best for you."

Ben laughed bitterly. "Including leaving me at Lisa's?"

"Leaving you?" Judy echoed. "But I came to see you every weekend."

"Yeah — that didn't last long," Ben said.

Judy stepped toward him. "Did you think I didn't want to come?" she said intensely. "Ben, the reason I stopped coming all the time was because it seemed to upset you so much. You hardly ever spoke to me. It seemed like you didn't want me around. I talked it over with Lisa, and we figured that it might be best if I gave you some space to settle in."

Amy saw the confusion in Ben's eyes. "But you always said it was your work." His voice, still angry, was now edged with uncertainty.

"That was just an excuse," Judy said. "I couldn't just stop coming without an explanation. It made it easier for me, that way."

Ben looked confused. "I've always believed it was your work. I thought it meant more to you than I did."

Judy stared at him. "Ben, nothing has *ever* meant more to me than you," she exclaimed. "I worked because I had nothing else in my life." Her voice suddenly shook.

"Having you was the best thing that ever happened to me. You're my son, and I love you."

There was a moment's silence. Slowly the confusion and hurt left Ben's face. "I didn't know, Mom," he said quietly. "Really, I didn't."

Mrs. Stillman reached out with both hands to Ben. He hesitated for a brief second, and then he stepped forward to hug her.

Amy and Soraya exchanged delighted grins.

Mother and son held each other for a long while. The moment was eventually broken by the sound of Red stamping his front hoof impatiently into the ground.

"I think Red's had enough of this sentimental moment," Judy said, pulling back from Ben with a smile.

Ben nodded. "Getting jealous, boy?" he said, patting the big chestnut.

Red tossed his head.

"Come on, let's get you back to the trailer." Ben smiled. "You get a break before the next round."

▬

There were ten horses in the jump-off. "So the fastest one wins?" Judy asked as Ben waited to go in the ring.

"The quickest round with the fewest penalty points," Ben explained. "But I'm not going to hurry Red. He's still young, and I'd prefer he jumped a clear round than rush it and knock down a load of fences. We've been working on keeping a steady pace at home. I don't want him to get overexcited and forget what he's learned. There'll be plenty of time for him to build up speed when he's more experienced. I'm just happy he made it in the jump-off."

Amy had to agree with Ben. She hated it when people raced young horses before they were ready. She thought Ben was smart to take it one step at a time. It would make Red a better jumper in the end.

The horse before Ben came trotting out of the ring. "Good luck!" Amy and Soraya called before going back to the stands with Judy.

Red tossed his head and snorted as he came into the ring and saw the jumps. He was obviously excited, but Ben kept to his word, steadying him at the start before guiding him through a fast but careful, clear round. When Red cantered out of the arena, his ears were pricked and his eyes confident.

"It was perfect — just the round I wanted," Ben said happily to the others as they hurried to congratulate him afterward.

"You were fantastic!" Amy exclaimed, feeding Red a mint from her pocket.

And it was enough to earn Red a yellow ribbon for third place. Only two other horses jumped clear, the rest completing fast rounds but gaining penalty points after knocking fences down. Amy, Soraya, and Judy watched proudly as Ben rode Red into the ring to collect his ribbon.

Amy turned happily to Soraya. "This has been a great day!" she said.

❧

As they untacked Red and got him ready for the journey home, Amy realized with a start how much colder it had become. Her breath froze in the air, and as she fastened the wraps on Red's legs, a few flakes of snow drifted down from the sky and landed on the nylon straps.

"You'd better get going," Judy said, helping Ben put his tack away. "It's coming in from the north, and the forecast said it would pick up toward nightfall."

"What are you going to do, Mom?" Ben asked.

"I was planning to head home," Judy said. "But looking at this weather, it might be best to find somewhere to stay around here for the night."

"You can stay at my place," Ben said quickly. "It's nothing special, but I have a fold-out bed."

Judy smiled at him. "That sounds perfect. I'll follow you back."

It didn't take long to get Red loaded up.

Amy, Ben, and Soraya climbed into the pickup. It was starting to get dark now. "I hope we get back before too much snow falls," Amy said, looking up at the ominously thick clouds as Ben started the engine and the wipers swept across the windshield.

"We don't have too far to go," Ben said.

"And it's not snowing that hard yet," Soraya pointed out. She smiled at Ben.

As Ben and Soraya talked happily about Red's performance in the jump-off, Amy watched the snowflakes falling through the dusk and thought about Melody. There had been no phone call from her grandpa, which must mean that she was OK. Amy was relieved. The last thing they wanted was for Melody to go into labor if there was a heavy snowfall that night. The farm's winding drive could become impassable in deep snow.

As they drove north toward Heartland, Judy following, the snow started to fall more quickly, and the drifts on the sides of the roads became noticeably deeper. Amy couldn't remember the last time it had snowed so much so early in the autumn.

❧

Eventually, they turned up the drive to the farm, the truck's wheels crunching into the frozen snow.

"Looks like we got here just in time," Ben said.

The farmhouse door opened as they drove into the yard, and Grandpa came out. He looked relieved to see them. "I was just about to call you," he said. "I was worried about you getting back in this weather."

"It didn't start really falling until we were almost here," Amy said.

"Well, at least you're here now," Grandpa replied. "I've fed the horses and put their blankets on. There's feed waiting for Red in his stall."

"Thanks, Grandpa," Amy said gratefully. "How's Melody?"

"Just fine." Grandpa turned to Soraya. "Your mom's been on the phone," he said. "I think you'd better call her and let her know that you're back safely."

"Sure," Soraya said.

"I'll give you a lift home," Ben called as Soraya headed for the house. "It'll save your mom coming out."

Soraya smiled at him. "Oh, that would be great!"

Judy parked her car and got out. "This is Ben's mom," Amy explained to Grandpa. "She's staying with him tonight."

"Pleased to meet you." Judy smiled at Grandpa.

"Why don't you come and wait inside while Ben gets things put away?" Grandpa offered.

Amy helped Ben unload Red and settle him into his stall. "I'll unbraid him for you," Amy offered. "You should head out before the snow gets any worse."

"Are you sure?" Ben said.

"Of course, no problem," she replied.

Ben went up to Red. "'Bye, big fella," he said softly. "You were the best today." The chestnut snorted and nuzzled his head against his owner's chest. Ben rubbed his forehead and then turned and smiled at Amy. "Thanks for all your help today."

"My pleasure," Amy said. "See you tomorrow."

She waved good-bye as Soraya, Ben, and his mom got into the pickup, and then she went back to Red's stall. She had just taken out the first braid when Grandpa appeared with a mug of chicken soup. "Here," he said. "You must be starving."

"Thanks, Grandpa." Amy took it gratefully. She wrapped her fingers around the hot mug, savoring the warmth. It was impossible to take out braids with gloves on, and her hands were freezing.

"So how was the show?" Grandpa asked.

Amy told him about Red's success and also about how Ben had made peace with his mom. "They finally seem to have put the past behind them." She grinned.

"That's good," Grandpa said quietly. "There's nothing worse than a family at odds." Amy heard the sadness in his voice and knew what he was thinking.

"How — how's Lou been today?" she asked tentatively.

"She's been in her room most of the evening," Grandpa

said. "Though she did come out and help me feed the horses when it started to snow."

"Oh, that's good," Amy said, feeling encouraged.

"Except she didn't speak to me." Grandpa sighed. "She hasn't said a word to me all day." He suddenly looked old and tired. "I'm going to start dinner. Don't be out here too long."

Amy watched him go, wishing more than ever that there was something she could do to sort things out between him and Lou.

After unbraiding Red, Amy brushed out the horse's mane and then left him to a well-earned rest. She checked on all the other horses and then went down to the house. Lou only made a brief appearance at dinner and didn't even talk much to Amy, disappearing to her room again as soon as the plates were cleared. Amy sat with Grandpa in the warmth of the kitchen, watching TV while the snow continued to fall outside.

At ten o'clock, Amy reluctantly got up from her chair. "I'm going to check on Melody again," she said to Grandpa.

"I'm sure she'll be fine," Jack replied.

But Amy knew she wouldn't be happy unless she made sure. She pulled on her boots, thick coat, and gloves and stepped outside. Snow swirled around her and a freezing wind bit into her cheeks. Shivering with cold, she fought her way through the drifts and up to the back barn.

Snow had piled up outside the doors, and she had to get a shovel to clear it. With a great effort, she heaved the door open and staggered into the quiet warmth of the barn. Sighing with relief, she shut the door behind her and felt for the light switch. As the lights lit up the darkness, she heard a few surprised snorts and rustles from the stalls.

She hurried down the aisle. "How are you, girl?" she said as she looked over Melody's door.

The words died on her lips. Melody was standing in her stall, her head down, her tail swishing. Damp patches of sweat stood out on her sides. Just then, a groan erupted from her and she sank to her knees. Amy caught sight of the beginnings of an opaque sac protruding from under Melody's tail and gasped.

Forgetting about the cold, Amy turned and raced back up the aisle and out of the barn. Stumbling and tripping she ran, half-blinded, through the snow.

"Grandpa!" she shouted, bursting into the kitchen. "Come quick! Melody's having her foal!"

Chapter Ten

Grandpa was on his feet almost before the words had left Amy's mouth. "What? Now?" he exclaimed.

"Yes!" Amy gasped. "I could see the sac coming out of her."

Grandpa strode into the hall. "Lou!" he shouted. "It's an emergency." He began to pull on his coat and hat. "Where's the foaling kit, Amy?"

"In the tack room," Amy said. "Should I call Scott?"

Before Grandpa could answer, Lou came running into the kitchen. "What is it?" she asked, her eyes flying from Amy to Grandpa. "What happened?"

"Melody's having her foal early," Grandpa said, going to the door. "Can you get in touch with Scott? I'm going up to the stall with Amy."

Lou grabbed the phone, her argument with Grandpa

seemingly forgotten in her desire to help. As she punched in the number, she asked, "Do you need anything else?"

"Boil some water and bring it up to the stall," Grandpa said.

"Sure." Lou nodded as Grandpa strode outside.

Amy ran after him, and together they fought their way through the blizzard, stopping only in the tack room to collect the foaling kit.

"I hope this is going to be a regular foaling," Grandpa shouted as they stepped out into the wind and snow again. "Scott's going to find it hard to get through to us in this!"

Amy's heart was pounding so fast that she thought it was going to burst. "Come on, Grandpa! We have to hurry!" she said.

They reached the barn, its electric lights shining out like a beacon into the darkness. Amy ran down the aisle, hugging the foaling kit against her ribs. She could hear Grandpa behind her.

"She's still down!" She gasped as Grandpa caught up with her at Melody's door.

The chestnut mare was lying in the straw, groaning as her sides heaved with a fresh contraction. Amy reached for the door bolt, but Grandpa stopped her.

"We'd better stay out here," he said in a low voice. "Animals don't like being disturbed when they're giving birth. If we go in, it might upset her. As long as there aren't any complications, she's better off on her own."

Amy looked at Melody's hindquarters. More of the opaque bag — the amniotic membrane that covered the foal — could be seen pushing through, under Melody's tail.

"The front hooves are out," Grandpa said, nodding toward the bag. "That's a good sign. The foal must be facing the right way."

Amy looked more closely and could see what he meant. She could make out two tiny hooves through the protective covering of the bag.

Melody's sides heaved again, and the hooves and front legs slid out a little more.

"Will we see the muzzle soon?" Amy asked.

Grandpa nodded. "It should come right after the front legs."

They watched as Melody continued to strain, but nothing happened. No muzzle appeared. Melody continued to groan.

"What's happening? Why's the head not coming?" Amy asked Grandpa anxiously.

Jack shook his head. "I don't know." Wrinkles of concern creased his forehead. "I hope it's not a malpresentation."

"What's that?" Amy asked quickly.

"It's when the foal isn't lying correctly," Jack explained. "The head is bent back either along the back or through the front legs. If that happens, the foal gets stuck and can't be born. If it *is* a malpresentation, Melody's going to need help."

Just then, the barn door opened, and Lou walked in with a covered bucket of water.

"Did you get through to Scott?" Grandpa said.

"Yes," Lou replied, quickly heading toward them, "but he says all the roads around here are blocked. He's already had another call that he couldn't get to."

Amy's eyes flew to her grandpa's face. "What are we going to do?" she asked.

"I'm going to have to find out what's holding up the foal," Grandpa said quickly. He shrugged off his coat and began to empty the equipment out of the foaling bucket. "Can you find me the antiseptic soap, Amy?"

"What's wrong?" Lou asked as Grandpa tipped some of the hot water into the bucket that had held the foaling kit. He began to soap his hands and arms.

"Grandpa thinks the foal's stuck," Amy said, so worried that she was hardly able to get the words out.

"But that's serious, isn't it?" Lou said.

Grandpa nodded and went into the stall. "It's OK, girl," he murmured to the mare. Hearing his footsteps, Melody looked around, her eyes wide and alarmed. As he approached, she began to try to struggle to her feet.

Jack quickly backed off. "I think she's going to panic if I get too close," he said.

"I'll hold her," Amy said.

"She might not let you," Jack said. "She'll be in so much pain, she won't be thinking straight."

"Let me try," Amy said.

She saw Grandpa nod and went quietly into the stall. Hearing the rustle of the straw, Melody's head shot into the air. "It's OK, girl, it's only me," Amy whispered.

Melody's head stayed high, but she didn't try to stand up. Her ears flickered as Amy slowly approached. "Steady now," Amy murmured. She knelt down beside the mare's shoulder and began to move her fingers in quick, light circles over Melody's damp skin. Although she desperately wanted Grandpa to be able to find out what was wrong as soon as possible, she forced herself to control her movements.

"You've got to let us help you," she said softly as her hands worked. Gradually, she felt the mare start to relax. She slowly worked her fingers up Melody's neck toward her head and ears. As she worked, she moved around until she was kneeling in front of the mare. With a sigh, Melody dropped her muzzle into her lap.

"I think she'll be OK now," Amy said softly, glancing over her shoulder to where Lou and Grandpa stood by the door. They both looked pale and worried.

After scrubbing up again, Grandpa came quietly into

the stall. Melody's eyes flickered uneasily, but she didn't move. Trying to keep her own breathing regular because she knew it would help to calm the mare, Amy started to work in small circles on her ears, her fingers stroking and soothing.

Grandpa approached quietly, and then, crouching down in the straw, he inserted his arm inside the mare. He felt around for a few minutes and let out a frustrated sigh.

"What's the matter, Grandpa?" Lou asked quickly.

"The foal's head is bent back along its sides," Grandpa said. "I was afraid of this." He straightened up and went back out of the stall to wash his arm. "It's stuck fast in the birth canal."

"So, what do we do?" Lou asked.

Grandpa's face was serious. "We need to turn the head. The problem is, it's so far back I don't think I can reach it." Amy saw the lines of worry etched along his face. "I'm going to have to call Scott and see what he thinks."

He hurried out of the barn. Amy looked at her sister. "Oh, Lou, is she going to be okay?" she said.

"I don't know," Lou replied. She looked around. "Would it be a good idea if I put this straw down?" she asked. "I guess we should have the bed as clean as possible."

Amy nodded. "Do you want me to help?"

Lou's eyes flickered to Melody. "No, you stay there."
She worked quietly. Melody groaned again.

Feeling close to tears, Amy kissed the mare's face. "It's going to be OK," she whispered. "It is!"

They heard the barn door open, and Grandpa appeared in the doorway. "What did Scott say?" Lou asked quickly.

Jack's face was serious. "We have to turn the foal around," he said.

"But I thought you said you couldn't reach it," Lou said.

"There isn't a choice," Jack said grimly. "If I can't reach the muzzle and turn it, we'll lose both Melody and the foal."

Amy felt the blood rush from her face. "They'll die?" she whispered.

Jack nodded. "Scott says there's no chance he can get through." He stripped off his coat and shirt again. "We have to do this ourselves."

Amy heard him plunge his arm into the bucket again.

Melody's sides contracted, and Amy caught back a sob. *Please, please don't die*, she prayed, seeing the pain and distress in the mare's eyes.

Grandpa came into the stall and inserted his arm inside Melody again.

Forcing herself to focus, Amy worked on the mare's ears to help settle her. However, by now Melody seemed to be past caring about Grandpa. Her breathing was hoarse, and her neck was soaked in sweat.

For what seemed like ages, Jack struggled to get a hold on the foal's head. "I can't get hold of it," he gasped. "If I could just hook my little finger in the corner of its mouth, then maybe I could turn its head around, but I just can't reach."

"Keep trying, Grandpa," Lou said, her eyes scared.

Amy looked anxiously at Melody. The mare was starting to tire. What if they were too late?

"It's no use!" Grandpa said, after five more minutes.

"You can't give up!" Amy said.

"I don't think there's anything more I can do," Jack said desperately.

The next minute, Lou entered the stall. "You can do it, Grandpa," she urged, kneeling down beside him. "I know you can."

Jack took a deep breath and reached deep inside Melody again. His face contorted as he struggled to get hold of the foal's muzzle.

"Come on," Lou whispered.

Amy saw their grandpa's face crease as he stretched his arm with one last enormous effort. "Got it!" he gasped suddenly. "I've reached its mouth."

Amy caught her breath, hope flooding through her as Grandpa began to ease the foal's head around, inch by difficult inch.

She bent her head to Melody's. *Please, please, please*, she prayed frantically. *Please be OK*.

"That's it!" Grandpa exclaimed suddenly, collapsing back onto the straw.

"I can see its nose!" Lou gasped. The mare's sides heaved with new force. "And here's its whole head!"

"She's tiring — she's going to need a hand," Grandpa said, struggling to his feet. "Lou, help me. We need to take hold of the front legs just above the fetlock joints, and pull as she pushes."

Lou did as he asked. Melody's sides shook in another contraction. "Pull now!" Grandpa cried.

Amy saw their faces grimace with effort as they both pulled. She had been holding her breath for so long now that she felt as if she was going to pass out.

Melody groaned.

"Here it comes!" Grandpa gasped. "Pull, Lou!"

Suddenly the foal's damp body slid out onto the straw.

Amy's heart almost stopped. "Is it OK?" she whispered, not knowing now whether to be relieved it was out or terrified by the foal's stillness.

Being careful not to break the umbilical cord that attached the foal to Melody, Grandpa bent over to examine it. As he did so, Amy saw the foal's tiny ears flicker and its head move.

"It's alive!" she cried, relief sweeping over her like a wave.

"Oh, Grandpa!" Lou exclaimed, flinging her arms around Jack.

He grinned happily. "Exhausted but alive," he said.

The tension in the stall dissolved. Grandpa stood with his arms around Lou while Amy stroked Melody's face, and they watched the foal start to move in the straw. It was perfect. A tiny, chestnut replica of Melody with a white blaze on its forehead. First, its eyes blinked open, and then it struggled onto its chest, its legs breaking through the membrane that still coated its body. As it struggled and kicked, the umbilical cord broke, and the foal took its first breath of real air.

Grandpa grabbed the iodine, cotton wool, and antibiotic powder from the foaling kit and quickly dressed the umbilical stump while the foal was still lying down.

"It's a filly," he said with a smile. "A little girl."

Suddenly, Amy felt Melody's nose move in her lap. Lifting her head, the exhausted mare looked around. Her ears pricked as she saw the foal. Amy hesitated for a moment and then edged away and joined Grandpa and Lou at the stall door.

Grandpa put his arm around her, and together they watched mother and foal meet each other for the first time.

Melody struggled to her feet. Blowing down her nose, she sniffed all over the filly with loud snorts. The foal snorted back, her tiny nostrils opening wide, her bedraggled ears pricking clumsily. Melody nuzzled the foal's damp face and then began to lick its coat.

"They're bonding," Grandpa said softly.

Happy tears filled Amy's eyes. "I can't believe they both survived," she said. She turned to Grandpa. "And it's all thanks to you."

"Thanks to *all* of us," Jack said, looking at her and Lou.

"But it was your determination, Grandpa," Lou said. "You were the one who wouldn't give up."

Amy saw an expression almost like regret cross Grandpa's face as he nodded. "I've always been stubborn," he said.

There was a pause. "Then I guess that makes two of us," Lou said softly, looking at her grandpa's worn features. "I knew you didn't mean to hurt me, Grandpa. I'm sorry I've been holding it against you."

"It's OK, Lou," Grandpa said. He looked at them both. "You two mean more to me than anything," he said. "Hurting you is the last thing I'd want to do. Please forgive me."

"Of course, Grandpa. If you'll forgive *me*," Lou said as he wrapped his arm around her shoulder.

"Thank goodness!" Amy said with a deep sigh of relief. It looked like the argument had finally been resolved.

"Oh, Amy," Jack said, looking at her. "Sorry you've been caught in the middle of all this."

"I'm just glad you finally worked it out," Amy said truthfully. She joined in the embrace. "You guys are the most stubborn people in the world."

Grandpa and Lou looked at each other.

"Well, apart from you," Lou said.

They all laughed. "Come on," Grandpa said as they separated. "Let's go inside. Melody and the foal will be just fine now."

"I think I'll stay for a little bit longer," Amy said, glancing at the foal. "Just until she gets up."

"OK," Grandpa said, nodding with understanding. "But don't try to help — it's important that she learns to stand on her own."

"We'll see you later," Lou said.

Amy leaned over the entrance to the stall and listened to the barn door banging shut behind them. Feeling totally drained, she sank down in the straw and looked at the chestnut filly lying there, her long limbs so tiny but perfect, the white blaze streaking down her forehead. There was only one more problem to be solved. "What shall we call you?" Amy whispered.

The little filly looked at her, her dark eyes bright.

Melody snorted softly, and suddenly the foal began to make her first attempt to stand. Stretching out her long, spindly legs, she got halfway to her feet and then collapsed into the straw with a soft thud. Amy longed to help her, but she knew Grandpa was right, it was a lesson the foal had to learn on her own.

With a toss of her head, the filly tried again. Her legs stretched and braced, and then with a heave she was on her feet. She wobbled for a second and fell over.

"Come on," Amy urged under her breath. "You can do it!"

The filly rested in the straw for a few minutes, and then Melody nudged her side. Out came the foal's legs again. She paused, a look of determination on her face, and then she struggled to stand. Her legs braced, she swayed a little, but this time she stayed on her feet. For a few moments, she just stood there, wobbling slightly. Then with a quick wag of her fluffy tail, she took an uncertain step forward and thrust her muzzle under Melody's belly.

Melody nuzzled her flank, and the filly began to feed.

Amy smiled and leaned her head back against the wall, shutting her eyes. It had been a long day, but at last, everything was OK.

🙊

Several hours later, she awoke with a start. She looked around and everything came flooding back. Melody and the foal were safe. They were lying in the straw, the foal's head resting against Melody's side.

Glancing at her watch, Amy saw that it was six o'clock. She'd been in the stall all night.

Feeling stiff, she got slowly to her feet. The foal's eyes blinked open and she raised her head, her tiny ears twitching.

Amy stood still. "It's all right," she murmured. "Stay there."

The foal looked at her for a long moment, and then with a sigh, she dropped her muzzle and shut her eyes again.

Amy crept out of the stall and shut the door as quietly as she could. There would be plenty of time to get to know the foal later in the day, but right now, she knew that Melody and her baby needed to rest. Stretching her cramped muscles, she walked to the barn door. Then, taking hold of the handle, she braced herself for the blizzard outside. As she pushed it open, she heard nothing but the silence of the morning.

As she stepped out, her boots crunched into the deep snow. The blizzard had stopped. The air was still, and in the night sky above, a tapestry of stars glittered. Amy shut the door and took a deep breath of the clear, cold air. Silence surrounded her — intense, deep, and peaceful.

Amy looked around at the buildings and fields of Heartland spread out before her. Everything was covered in a blanket of thick snow. As she looked toward the east, she saw the first pale gray glimmers of daybreak creeping across the dark sky, and suddenly she knew what Melody's filly should be called.

"Daybreak," she whispered. For a new beginning and the start of a new life.